M000282474

THE MAN WITH
SIX SENSES

THE MAN WITH SIX SENSES

MURIEL JAEGER

with an introduction by
MIKE ASHLEY

This edition published 2020 by
The British Library
96 Euston Road
London
NW1 2DB

Originally published in 1927 by The Hogarth Press

The Man with Six Senses © 1927 The Estate of Muriel Jaeger
Introduction © 2020 Mike Ashley

"Muriel Jaeger's Educated Woman and the New Nativity Narrative"
from *Dangerous by Degrees*, New Brunswick: Rutgers University Press, 1989,
© 1989 by Susan J. Leonardi. Reprinted by permission of Rutgers University Press.

This novel is presented as it was originally published and as such contains language in
common usage at the time of its writing. Neither the publisher nor the contributors
endorse any language which would now be considered xenophobic or offensive.

Cataloguing in Publication Data
A catalogue record for this book is available from the British Library

ISBN 978 0 7123 5366 3
e-ISBN 978 0 7123 6745 5

The photograph of Muriel Jaeger on page 6 of this edition is also
reproduced with the permission of the Estate of Muriel Jaeger.

The front cover illustration and frontispiece feature a detail of a clematis stem as
viewed through a microscope in *The Wonders of the Microscope photographically revealed
by means of Olley's Patent Micro-Photographic Reflecting Process*, London, 1857–61.

Front cover design by Jason Anscomb

Typeset by Tetragon, London
Printed in England by CPI Group (UK) Ltd, Croydon, CR0 4YY

CONTENTS

INTRODUCTION

Powers of the Mind

The idea that we may all have latent powers of the mind—telepathy, clairvoyance, telekinesis and so on—has been around for centuries. In the Greek legends Cassandra, daughter of Priam, king of Troy, had the power of prophecy. The Gorgons, most notably Medusa, could turn people to stone with the power of their eyes—this developed into the belief long-held by many cultures of the "evil eye." In the New Testament, Luke tells how Jesus could cure the sick by laying his hands on them.

Some of these ideas came into focus through the thinking of Franz Mesmer in the late 1770s who believed that all living things had a form of animal magnetism which allowed for a transfer of natural energy. This later became called mesmerism and later still, hypnotism.

The idea of mesmerism soon entered fiction. There is a suggestion of it in *Wieland* (1798) by Charles Brockden Brown, usually regarded as the first American gothic novel. The sinister Carwin is accused of influencing people's actions through some projection of his voice. E. T. A. Hoffmann, Edgar Allan Poe, Lord Lytton and others were fascinated with the idea of mesmerism—Poe went so far as to suggest it could keep a human's mind active even after the body had died in "The Facts in the Case of M. Valdemar" (1845).

The most famous story of mesmeric or hypnotic power is undoubtedly *Trilby* (1895) by George Du Maurier. The young model, Trilby, who has a lovely voice but is tone deaf, is hypnotised by the musician Svengali to be able to sing and perform perfectly. Trilby is totally under his spell. The book was so popular that the very name Svengali entered the language for anyone who has a sinister control over others.

Powers of the mind soon stretched beyond animal magnetism to include any extra-sensory perception, and when the Society for Psychical Research was established in 1882, one of their purposes was to study that subject. By then the idea that anyone had the power to read others' thoughts was suggestive of a higher form of mental or perhaps even supernatural ability. Edward Bulwer-Lytton, who had already given mesmerism an occult tinge in *A Strange Story* (1861) gave it and telepathy a more scientific basis in *The Coming Race* (1871). Lytton depicts an underground society that draws its energy and power from an electromagnetic force called *vril*. This incorporates electricity, radiation and magnetism and allows the Vril-ya to control minds and read thoughts. This was much the same as the odic or life-force that had been suggested by the German philosopher Baron von Reichenbach in 1845.

Whatever the forces or powers, natural or supernatural, people who could use them were generally regarded with suspicion and in fiction, as with Svengali, they were usually up to no good. In the apocalyptic novel, *The Crack of Doom* (1895), Robert Cromie's villain, who is intent upon conquering the power of the atom and thereby destroying the Earth, was telepathic and bends various characters to his will.

It was unusual, therefore, to create a character who had any extra-sensory powers but whom the reader would regard with sympathy. J. D. Beresford was the first to attempt this in *The Hampdenshire Wonder* (1911) where we encounter Victor Stott, a young lad regarded as a "hydrocephalic idiot" but who in reality has an advanced intellectual capacity. On first encountering him, people believe he has the evil eye and they are frightened because of his malevolent stare. Beresford nevertheless shows the child's loneliness and inevitable fate and raises the question of whether, despite our fear of Stott, he may have been an example of the next step in human evolution.

The person who took this theme one step further was Muriel Jaeger in *The Man with Six Senses*, published in 1927. This is the story of Michael Bristowe, a young boy with a developing sense of psychic awareness. He is looked after by Hilda, who starts out as something of a mother figure to young Michael. The story is narrated by Ralph Standring, who is in love with Hilda and so resents Michael, who is taking up too much of Hilda's time and attention. Michael is also resentful of his talent, and hostile towards those who do not believe he has an ability, and that it is some kind of party trick. As a consequence we see Michael mostly as an outcast not only of society but of himself. It is a formidable study of a boy isolated by his own natural abilities.

Jaeger liked the concept of the outcast. They feature in all her fiction, especially *The Question Mark* (1926) where a man is projected into the future. Though he befriends a family he fails to find a place in this new world and remains forever the outsider looking in. It is the same with Michael Bristowe. He finds it difficult to come to terms with his talent and to convince others it is genuine. Hilda explains this to Ralph at one key point early in the book:

"...You see, one likes to play sometimes with the idea
of one's own exceptional personality, but have you ever
considered how appalling it would be to discover that one
really was abnormal in some important way?"

Muriel Jaeger (1892–1969) came from a fairly well-to-do middle-
class Yorkshire family. She had literary ambitions even while at
High School in Sheffield, publishing poetry in the school maga-
zine. She obtained a scholarship to Oxford University where
she studied at Somerville College. There she began a lasting
friendship with Dorothy L. Sayers and was later instrumental
in encouraging Sayers to write her first Lord Peter Wimsey
novel. During the war she served in the Ministry of Food which
focused her mind on the need for controlled agriculture, an
idea that forms part of the new world in *The Question Mark*.
She turned to writing after the war, obtaining her diploma in
journalism in 1920. In addition to being the sub-editor of the
weekly paper *Time and Tide*, run by Lady Rhondda, she wrote
four other novels that saw publication and possibly as many
as ten novels that were never published. *The Question Mark*
was her first and, as with *The Man with Six Senses*, was published by Leonard and Virginia Woolf in their Hogarth Press
imprint. After a gap of some years, when she had turned to
writing non-fiction and works for the theatre, she completed
Hermes Speaks (1933), another foray into the world of a gifted
and manipulated child, and *Retreat from Armageddon* (1936),
a rather more philosophical book as a group of individuals
retreat from a global war into a country house to discuss the
failings of mankind. Her fascination with how lives develop was
explored in *Experimental Lives* (1932) where she studied people

who lived their own lives by their own plans rather than by the demands of society. Jaeger continued to write almost up to her death, but she did not return to the world of the scientific romance, even though it is this world that still remembers her and celebrates her work.

MIKE ASHLEY

THE MAN WITH
SIX SENSES

I

THIS IS NOT THE ACCOUNT OF MICHAEL BRISTOWE'S strange career that Hilda asked me to write. I have not begun that account yet, though Hilda put the matter to me urgently the last time I saw her before I sailed a week ago. Hilda has a trick of making the most heart-rending demands upon one, not because she is cruel, but because she is young and innocent—"unawakened," as a Victorian novelist would have said. But this record I make from purely egoistic motives, in the hope that so I may spiritually work through the whole thing again and put it behind me, since I have now made up my mind to free myself completely from the coil of circumstances and emotions which has made the last few years of my life a wretched and confused futility. I am a literary man, and I know that this is the right remedy for my disease—the lancing of the abscess. I do it, therefore, for my own sake. Michael Bristowe may have been all that Hilda thought—a portent and a promise—a being of racial importance. But, when all is said, a man still owes something to himself.

Every day England is farther behind me, and that is to the good. Nevertheless, this period of inevitable idleness before adventure is trying to body and mind, and, for me, shipboard distractions are not enough. I am not now so young that mere blue water and movement, concerts, sports and promenade-deck flirtations can rid me of the obsession that has been holding me for years. I must step up to it again, pull the hood off its ugly grinning face, look at it till I know it, look till I know all there is to be known about it, go on looking until it begins to bore me. And then I shall be able to turn away and forget about it for ever.

Later, if necessary, I can extract from this the sort of formal attestation that Hilda wanted. All the facts will be here. But this account no one will ever see—unless, perhaps, Hilda herself some day—but where would be the use of that? No one will ever see it.

Hilda made her request to me on perfectly rational grounds (as, of course, Hilda would be certain to), because, besides being a professional writer, I had seen a good deal of Michael Bristowe during these last few years, had been present on several significant occasions, and believed in his surprising faculty and its potentialities. Not that any open-minded person who saw anything at all of him could have withheld belief. But then there are so few open-minded people. Most people's beliefs are so teleological. They are decided by what they are to lead to, not by what they start from. Old Rosenheimer's remark at that first interview was typical:

"Gold and copper exactly alike!" I can hear his laugh now—it was not a musical one. "Gold and copper exactly alike! That's not much good to a business man, you know!"

"Not exactly alike." I remember how Michael's black brows drew together. He was keeping his temper only because he had promised Hilda that he would. "Very nearly. One—I—can't distinguish them at a distance, if there is something in between. Not at present. Perhaps I may be able to some day when I have had more practice."

"Then come back when you can, young man, come back when you can." Rosenheimer turned his great wide back upon us, still shaking with laughter. "Till then, you'll stick to your water-divining, if you take my advice."

I had realised early in the interview that Rosenheimer was not taking the matter seriously, and I was fuming inwardly in the knowledge that I had been placed in a false position. Hilda had used indirectly a little influence to get Bristowe this interview with the big man of the Westralian Mining Syndicate, and she had used her influence with me to make me act as Bristowe's sponsor. I had not been enthusiastic, and neither (as it now appeared) had Rosenheimer. We had both been pushed into it. And Michael was, as usual, sullenly shy, on the alert for mockery and hostility. It is hardly surprising that the occasion was not a success.

Rosenheimer had been jocose from the beginning. I think he regarded water-divining as something of the same nature as fortune-telling and table-turning. I knew a little better than that—"dowsing" is common enough in our part of the country—but I had, none the less, some sympathy for the big man's attitude. I knew that, however thoroughly the existence of the faculty was established, it was of very uncertain utility. I was prepared to take Hilda's word that Michael Bristowe had to an unusual degree this queer instinct which warned him of the presence of underground water and of mineral deposits, but I strongly doubted whether he would ever find it of much practical value to him.

To me, at that moment, Bristowe was merely one of the untrained, unwanted, derelict youngsters who encumbered the world so embarrassingly in the years following the Great War.

One was impelled to try to find niches for them, if only for one's own mental comfort; but, again, it seemed so impossible a task that one might almost be pardoned for ignoring it altogether. And young Bristowe was not even "ex-Service." He had substituted a bad attack of pneumonia and a long spell of ill-health for the two years' active service he might otherwise have had. That was now an additional handicap in finding ordinary employment for him. If, therefore, the youth really had an unusual gift and something could be done with it, so much the better, I had decided. And I am afraid I was not altogether innocent of the further idea that, if the employment of his gift involved emigration to Australia, that would be so much the better too. It had seemed to me odd and unnecessary that Hilda should have taken up this particular surplus youth. But as she was obviously committed now to "see him through," seen through he must be as quickly as possible. As things were, he was a nuisance.

I had come home intending to see a good deal of Hilda—that is, if she still corresponded to the impression I had received of her during that last Christmas leave which I had passed in my West-country home before demobilisation. My mother had wanted me to propose marriage to Hilda then and there, but I was not ready. For four and a half years, though comparatively well off in my staff job, I had done what I did not choose and gone where I would not, and now, like other young men, I wanted my good time. My own sort of good time I wanted, and that had nothing to do with dancing, nor revue, nor night-clubs, nor the swopping of motor-bicycles. It implied a suave and soothing year or two of Italian sunshine, where I might try to woo back to life the little book of literary and æsthetic essays which had been one of the earliest victims of the mailed fist.

Besides, at that time, Hilda herself had been obviously too young, the right woman for me (I recognised it even then), but not ready any more than I was. My mother did not see that. In her young days, eighteen or nineteen had still been considered a very suitable age for a girl's marriage. She did not understand, nor accept, our later maturing, due to the increasingly complicated demands of civilised and cultured life, which make a longer period of growth essential if a completely adequate personality is to emerge.

Hilda was lovely then, as she still is, even after all that has happened. I used to imagine her as the young heroine of an old Teutonic epic or of an Icelandic saga. I know that her grandmother came from the Orkneys, and I can very well believe that Hilda has Norse blood in her veins. Nothing has ever given me greater æsthetic pleasure than the presenting of her as a Viking princess in the acting that we had at Marling that last Christmas. She looked the part so exquisitely with her tall, lithe body, her shining fairness, and her brown hair, with its gleam ruddier than mere Saxon blondeness, hanging in two thick braids over her shoulders.

She looked noble that night, but she looked very, very young—a noble child. I decided then that I would not propose to her yet, in spite of my mother's urgency. We both needed more time. Some day, probably two or three years hence, when I had written my book and Hilda had finished her college career, I would fall in willingly enough with what I suspected to be a long-standing family plot.

This suspicion did not make me resentful. My mother's tastes and mine had always agreed very well, and I am never inclined to rebel for the mere sake of rebelling—though it is possible that the sense that I had always been expected to marry Hilda made me the more determined to choose my own time for it. That my mother might not, in that case, live to see it, never occurred to me, for there was nothing then to suggest the sudden illness which led to her death a year later. Her chief preoccupation in the affair was that I should marry into a "good" family, now that I was the only surviving son. A young cousin of mine had committed matrimonial suicide not long before, during one of those demoralising short leaves. It had not been the proverbial barmaid, but a specimen of sub-urban gentility with a manner of speech like that of an actress in musical comedy—a type, if possible, even more difficult.

I was aware that this disaster was always in the background of my mother's mind, as she urged me prematurely into the bonds of matrimony, and it irritated me that she should under-stand me so little. She should have known that her son was too much like herself, had too strongly her own sense of fitness, her artist's eye, to commit an incongruity of that sort; I have had my follies, like other people, but they have stopped short of that. I was tempted into a teasing attitude, which I have since regretted. I, on my side, should have known better than to expect too much insight from her; she was an artist, a crafts-woman in the art of comely living, not a psychologist, and her anxiety for the charming fabric of life that she had helped to create at Marling was natural. It was not that she was a snob; her touchstone was always a man's behaviour, as I hope it is also mine. Any workman, as she once said, was welcome to treat her as if he belonged to her class, so long as he did not treat her as if she belonged to his. It remains a fact that comely behaviour is more commonly found in those whose forbears have been gently bred than in the others. No less than my mother, I was pleased that Hilda should belong to the first category.

I was pleased also by a matter on which my mother reserved judgment—that Hilda was already preparing for a university career, and I did not want to do anything to interfere with it or unsettle her mind. I have never been against the higher education of women, as, openly or covertly, are many of my contemporaries. I think an educated man is all the better for having an educated wife, who is able to be an intellectual companion to him, to be interested in his work, and to follow the movements of his mind.

And so I went and had my few years in Italy, with only a brief interruption at the time of my mother's death. And the book of essays had returned according to plan, and had been published, and had a certain *succès d'estime*. And, not at all according to plan, I had had also a feverish love affair with an impulsive Neapolitan whose household was distinct from that of her husband. But that was over now and, in the reaction, I had felt a longing for green England and the clipped speech of my countrymen, and had thought once or twice very pleasantly of Hilda's cool fairness and of her fresh young mind and body.

In fact, there is no doubt that I had idealised Hilda a little during those last months in Italy, when I was clearing up there my affairs, material and emotional, not without some exacerbation, and it was perhaps inevitable that the reality should fall short of my expectations.

There had been a touch of shy timidity about the old Hilda that I had found very attractive, even though it had emphasised the immaturity of which I have spoken. I saw at once that the tall self-possessed girl who welcomed me so graciously in the

pleasantly austere sitting-room had just that little additional
confidence, that social aplomb, which I had counted on her
gaining during the past few years. And yet, perversely, I missed
the old shyness. I had followed her career at a distance during
these years. She had now lost both parents, like myself; but
the old family plot still occasionally showed signs of life, with
my energetic sister and the aunt who had been Hilda's guardian as its principals; and I had never been left long without
news of Hilda. I knew that she had completed her university
career with high success; that in the meantime, as to so many
families, post-war retrenchment had become necessary, and
that she had immediately found a job as secretary to one of
the political women who hoped to be in the next Parliament.
Her old home had been let on lease, and her aunt had gone
abroad to the warmer climate that her health was beginning
to require. Hilda herself had taken a small flat in Bloomsbury
and, in modern fashion, was living there by herself. I knew all
this, but nevertheless I had not expected this new air in her of
being so very much upon her own ground. Since I am to write
the whole truth, I had not been entirely innocent of a vision of
myself arriving at this juncture as a possible welcome rescuer
from somewhat uncongenial circumstances.

I decided quickly, however, that any change in her was no
more than superficial. There was no dimming of the shining
quality that I remembered, that unconscious openness which
seems to symbolise itself most perfectly in the faces of very
fair young people. It is the quality that I suppose Pope Gregory
noticed that day when he saw the young northern barbarians
standing in the slave-market in Rome, and conceived a spiritual
father's yearning after their untaught souls. "Candour," the

splendid word that was so cruelly overworked in the eighteenth century that it finally fell into a decline, expresses best the quality I mean, and perhaps only those who have lived abroad for a time can appreciate the sheer beauty of candid young English faces. This, and its spiritual counterpart, the refreshment of utter honesty, one gets—I have always had—from Hilda. And, once one has found that, in this world of shams and subterfuges, perhaps one must be homesick for it ever afterwards.

Nevertheless the meeting was not quite what I had anticipated. I had sent Hilda my book, and she referred to it almost at once. She understood, evidently, that a writer does not want amateurs to criticise his methods, however flatteringly, but to show interest in his subject-matter. This pleased me, but I was almost taken aback by the aptness of her comments on some of my theses. I suppose that one is liable to forget as one grows older the possibilities of rapid mental development in the early twenties. It had not occurred to me that I might have to get to know Hilda all over again. It was a suggestion not entirely welcome to a man coming in search of solace.

And then, before I had had time to readjust my ideas, Michael Bristowe came in. That was unwelcome too. I did not recognise him at first, though I had a vague impression that I had seen him somewhere before; but I thought that Hilda might have kept this first evening free from interruption—I had let her know that I was coming. And when I realised a little later who Bristowe was, the knowledge did not soothe my irritation.

My recollection of him went back to my last year at Sandal, when he was a tiresome small boy recommended to my special care by my mother, with that reckless ignorance of schoolboy taboos and lines of social demarcation that mothers are apt to display.

The dialogue, as I remember it, took typical form.

"I hope you will help little Michael Bristowe to settle down at Sandal, Ralph. His mother was speaking to me about it the other day."

"He'll have to find his own feet. I can't do much."

"Well, do as much as you can, my son. His people are so nice and unassuming, and I believe they are making great sacrifices to send him there. He's a nervous little lad, too, so his mother says. She can never take him to church, because he's frightened of going through the graveyard—always turns sick, she says, though they are sure that no one has ever told him ghost stories. They hope school will help him to get over all that."

I smiled to myself, thinking that it probably would. Attacks of sickness or coughing or hiccoughs are not uncommon in school chapel among the junior boys, but they are not encouraged by the staff. But wasn't it like my luck, I thought, to be saddled with a "nervous little lad"?

As a fact, I did make one or two awkward casual attempts to "see about" young Bristowe, knowing that my mother, conscientious in such matters, would be certain to question me on the subject. But he was a shy and unpopular small boy, one of those morose solitaries to be found in every school and college, apparently incapable of making friends, or even of discovering any tolerable *modus vivendi* among his neighbours. I belonged myself to a rather dashing, artistic set in the Sixth, and, when my companions had laughed at me once or twice for running after the small, dirty, unprepossessing urchin, I must confess to abandoning the uncongenial obligation altogether.

I don't think I had seen young Bristowe from that day to this, and I had not known that Hilda knew him. His people lived in our local township, but we did not come across them socially. His father was a general practitioner in a small way, a clever surgeon, it was said, but marred by a bad habit not uncommon among doctors. Mrs. Bristowe, a local farmer's daughter, had probably required some courage when she approached my mother on Michael's behalf. I found later that Hilda's acquaintance with Michael was of quite recent date, the result of an accidental encounter during one of her long vacations.

I mean, as far as possible, to set down my impressions here as they occurred at the time, without the corrections or modifications which I might make in the light of after events. Only so can I re-live the whole experience, as I must, comprehend it as a whole, and at last consign it, finished, to oblivion. And, if I am to write in this way, I must say that, at this, my first sight of him in adult life, Bristowe struck me as hardly more prepossessing than in our schooldays. It was not that he was awkward of build, having a light, compact figure; and the snub-nosed, amorphous little face had certainly acquired significance since those old times. Yet, at first sight, and indeed, always, it was difficult to say precisely what that significance was. It was as one says to oneself sometimes before a work of art of a new and puzzling type—"I can see that this thing means something, but I cannot for the life of me see what it does mean." One could not ignore Michael Bristowe; his thick black brows and the sullen line of his mouth, and, perhaps, something more subtle than these, caught one's attention whether one wished it or not. But it was not, to me at least, a pleased attention. There was that old air of hang-dog moroseness, of being at odds with the world, which expresses itself more in the carriage of the figure and the poise of the head than in actual expression, and which, I truly believe, was what I had recognised in Bristowe at the first glance, when I felt that I had seen him before. And, to emphasise the effect, he had now also that furtive "unemployed" look about the eyes that we all came to know so well in those days. Sentimentalists are wrong in supposing that crime leaves its impression on the physiognomy. It is not the crime, it is the being found out. Undetected wife murderers have no difficulty in finding fresh wives to murder. I myself have had to do with one or two thieves at close quarters in my life. None of them was a particularly unprepossessing specimen—until they were found out. It was then that the criminal stigmata appeared. They became in a day hang-dog, furtive, leaden of complexion. Many of these post-war unemployed—especially those who remained unemployed for months and years—developed a similar appearance. They had been found out in the worst crime of the modern decalogue—that of commercial failure. Bristowe had this look. It seemed merely a psychological compensation that the boy's manner was apt to flaunt a kind of arrogant aloofness, almost at times bordering upon insolence.

He showed it when Hilda introduced him to me after they had exchanged a few sentences then incomprehensible to me.

"He's written," Bristowe had exclaimed at the moment of entering the room, a watchful half-smile at Hilda lighting up his dark face. "He wants me to go there to-morrow."

"Oh, Michael, I'm so glad!" Hilda had sprung up and gone to him, seizing without ceremony a letter which he had pulled from his pocket.

Bristowe watched her as she read, with the air of a perverse son who knows that he has done something that will please his mother, but is a little fearful at having so far committed himself.

"I'm so glad," said Hilda again, her eyes shining. "And here, in the nick of time, is Ralph Standring to help us with the business part of it."

"Oh, Standring and I have met before." Michael turned and stared at me as if he had only just seen me, and yet with immediate recognition. No doubt, I had changed less in the last twelve years than he. "We were at school together, weren't we?"

Then I remembered him, and the distasteful old association combined with the unwelcome new one. I did not like his tone, nor his careless turn-out, and the obviously familiar terms of his acquaintance with Hilda disconcerted me. Still less did I like the constant movements of his long white hands, which I then took to be an unwholesome nervous symptom. I thought he looked neurasthenic, a condition which I knew well enough, having seen many shell-shocked men. I decided on the spot that it must be one of my first cares to detach him from the girl who might very well become my wife.

And yet the grinning Providence which had intertwined my destiny with young Bristowe's gave its first ironical indication that evening. There was no avoiding it. Before I left Hilda's flat that night I was committed to see this undesirable young cub through his interview with the big mining magnate, just as I had been called upon to sponsor the "nervous little lad" at school twelve years before. And the eccentric grounds for the interview were that Bristowe had been found to be a "dowser" of unusual sensitiveness—I had to accept Hilda's account of how she had seen him at work—and could point out the location of underground minerals, even, so they said, without the help of the hazel twig that only the most expert operators can dispense with.

I comforted myself with the reflection that if we succeeded and Bristowe went abroad, the little problem would solve itself; otherwise, I would have a private conversation with Hilda without delay, and would mildly suggest how unnecessary it was to let an acquaintance of this kind extend itself indefinitely. Meanwhile, I would do my best, a more conscientious best than those abortive attempts at Sandal in the past.

And then, before we had been three minutes in old Rosenheimer's sanctum, I knew that the whole affair was futile. He questioned Michael in the half curious, half good-humouredly baiting tone in which one might question a gipsy fortune-teller. And when Michael said plainly that he could not distinguish the sensation which he received from buried gold from that which he received from buried copper, I knew that he had destroyed any forlorn chance he might have had of impressing the great man.

The boy had certainly no *savoir faire*. Having declared his inadequacy with quite unnecessary emphasis, he suddenly began to press with an eagerness that he had not shown before. It was evident that when he saw the opportunity actually slipping away, he abruptly realised how little he could afford to lose it. It would be difficult to imagine behaviour less likely to attract a prospective employer.

"Then you won't even give me a chance to show what I can do?" The demand had a disturbing shrillness.

"My dear young man"—Rosenheimer turned his smiling face to us again over his shoulder from the work-table where he had settled. He obviously considered the interview over, but, with the good-temper of his race, would humour us a little farther. "My dear young man, you have just said yourself you can't find gold to be sure of it—what possible value do you think you could be to us? No doubt you are a very clever young man; but, if I were you, I should find something a little more—shall we say?—practical, to do. If you care to ask at the office downstairs, if we have any vacancies for clerical work— I'll telephone down—" He glanced suggestively at the door.

"You're like all the rest," Michael thrust out, in a furious mutter. "You can't see an inch beyond the end of your nose. See!... Why, if you'd give me a chance—oh! what's the good of talking?"

The young man flung out of the room in what I could only call a thoroughly childish pet, and slammed the door behind him, leaving me uncomfortably "in the air." I flatter myself I am equal to most situations, but I did not enjoy this one. The least I could do was to apologise to Rosenheimer, and it did not improve my temper to see how the old money-spider relished my apology.

As I passed down the stairs after Bristowe, I thought I would see that youth far enough before I would undertake a job of this sort on his behalf again, even though Hilda asked it. I did not know then how little it depended upon anything I might decide how many or what sort of things I should come to do for Hilda.

I I

THE STRANGENESS OF MICHAEL BRISTOWE SLID INTO MY life with this amazing commonplaceness. It seemed to me at that time merely a small, but annoying, factor in my personal problem. "Neither will they be persuaded, though one rose from the dead." Is that the true description of my attitude? Am I indeed one of those who would have washed his hands of Christ, condemned Socrates, silenced Galileo? Even now, I am not sure who was right, Hilda or I. The thing is beyond me. I don't know whether it was important or trivial. I don't know whether Hilda was heroic or ridiculous. This I may say, in my excuse, if it be that I need one—we are not brought up to be easily impressed in these days. It is axiomatic, a matter of faith, with us, that everything is commonplace. We learn to regard any expression of awe, any acknowledgment of mystery, as the Red Indian regarded signs of pain under torture. Nothing unusual can happen to a modern man, for his reception of it immediately transmutes it into a complete banality. We fly through the air to our business interviews, we conduct newspaper controversies on Survival after Death, in which the controversy plainly becomes more important than the Survival; voices speaking to us from the other side of the globe are quite likely to be cut off because we cannot be bothered with them; "death rays" are a drug on the market. It is not surprising if a minor wonder passes almost unregarded.

Partly, I think, also, my attitude to Bristowe's peculiarity was due to the fact that Hilda herself was so quiet and practical about it. Of course, she had had time to get used to the idea. She presented it without excitement, though she presented it as significant. On the other hand, it was to my interest to minimise it, and I did minimise it. I found it easy to minimise it. That seems curious now. I ought to have taken it seriously from the first. Whatever its intrinsic value, it was certainly capable of having a decisive influence upon the course of my life. I pause to wonder whether, otherwise, I should even now have found it worthy of much consideration. It almost appears as if human reason were not so far developed as we commonly suppose, and that even a trained intelligence could still judge things only in an egocentric manner. One is Man, the latest product and protagonist of the Struggle for Existence, in the first place, and, only in the second, if at all, *homo sapiens*. I am, without boasting, a highly educated man, and I belong to a profession which has accustomed me to the investigation of external facts, and to introspection and criticism of my own mental processes. Yet I cannot be sure that in my judgment of this matter I was more disinterested than old Rosenheimer himself, with his "Gold and copper exactly alike! Ha! ha! ha!" or than any savage who ever made gods in his own image.

Thus, the circumstances under which I listened to Hilda's account of young Bristowe were such that I had a preoccupation—a positively adverse preoccupation; and, like those who go to Russia, I saw what I expected to see, and came back with my previous opinion confirmed.

I was entertaining Hilda to dinner at my Club. It was the Parthenon, a pleasant well-run place, used principally by literary men of established reputation, and sufficiently modernised without any degeneration towards Bohemianism. I had chosen it because it was this sort of place, because I wanted to present Hilda with a contrast to all that, to me, Michael Bristowe had represented, when I had seen him at her flat the week before. I wanted for her the psychological effect of panelled walls, shining silver, white napery, suave dress-suited diners and unobtrusively hovering waiters; of beautifully cooked and daintily served food, of choice wine. I thought that this would be a good preparation for what I had to say.

Looking back now, I find that conversation oddly symbolic and prophetic, and that, even though it began with a small verbal concession on Hilda's part:

"It's nice to be thoroughly civilised sometimes."

She herself was dressed in black with handsome quietness as apt to the atmosphere of the place as one could wish. There were few women in the room, since their presence as guests had only lately been sanctioned, and, of these, she was easily the one most likely to attract attention. It seemed in some way both admirable and pathetic that, all the time we sat there, she was obviously utterly unconscious of the discreetly admiring glances of my fellow-clubsmen.

I had not intended to talk of Bristowe much, nor at once. As I have said, I did not then take him very seriously. I thought that he was probably just a small social mistake on Hilda's part, such as all insufficiently guided young people are apt to make; and that he would be quite easily dealt with.

It vexed me a little when I found that Hilda supposed I had arranged this meeting especially in order to report on that abortive interview with old Rosenheimer. She told me that she knew I had done my best.

"I did my best," I repeated acidly, "and if the young man we were trying to help had also done his, perhaps the result might have been different."

And I gave my account of the meeting. It seemed to correspond sufficiently with the one she had already had from Bristowe himself.

"I think myself, you know," she added, "that Michael was quite creditably patient."

"Patient!"

"Yes. You know, Ralph, we mustn't forget that he is a remarkable person and has a remarkable gift."

I said, "The only remarkable thing I've seen about him so far is his remarkable perverseness."

Hilda listened to me gravely with a tiny frown. She seemed to be neither irritated nor amused by my sarcasm, merely reflective.

I cast about for a line to take.

"Don't you think," I said lightly at last, "that you may be taking this young man a little too seriously? No doubt, it is very pleasant and uncommon to be a water-diviner, but, after all, there are more important things. Common-sense, for instance, and making one's way in the world, and not being a nuisance to people—even, perhaps, good manners."

Hilda was still regarding me seriously, rather, I feared, to the detriment of the Parthenon's excellent dinner.

"Yes, Ralph," she said, "it is very much a question of relative importance. And, as you haven't seen Michael at work, you can't be expected to know what importance to attach to that."

"I don't particularly want to see him at work," I said hastily. "I've seen it all before. I'm willing to take your word for it that, like a number of other people, he can detect underground streams and deposits of ore. What I don't see is that it matters very much. The faculty is evidently not exact enough to be of commercial value, and anyhow, geological science has pretty well superseded it by this time. So why make all this song about it?"

By way of answer, Hilda suggested that she should tell me how she had come to know young Bristowe.

I agreed willingly. The talk was not taking the lines which I had sketched out for it; but it was already becoming clear to me that it was not going to be so simple as I had supposed to detach my undesirable young schoolfellow from Hilda Torrington. And if it was going to be difficult, the more light I could get on the nature of the problem the better.

It was in this spirit that I began to listen to what I now realise may well have been one of the strangest stories ever told by one human being to another. I wish now that I could have heard it freshly with an open mind, as told by a person whom I did not know about a person whom I did not know. If this could have been, the results might have been important—they might even have meant salvation for several people, including perhaps myself. I had money. At that early stage I could perhaps have relieved the pressure of a critical situation. Money can relieve most kinds of pressure directly or indirectly, especially now, in our highly civilised state, when not only food and clothing, but such things as light, air, space, cleanliness, time to think, have to be bought with it. It is often the lack of these latter that gives the last turn to the screw and produces the catastrophes of life. On the other hand, it is possible that nothing that I could have done then would have radically altered the situation. Events might well have followed a similar course to a similar conclusion.

Even as it was, Hilda's tale caught my interest in places. But my preoccupation—my personal situation—persisted and controlled my reception of it.

It seemed that Hilda's first meeting with Bristowe had occurred during the last of her long vacations rather more than a year before, at a farm-house on the Torrington land. The farm was kept by a childless old couple who had known Hilda all her life, and who had a loyal affection for her of that ancient half-feudal type for the passing of which England is so much the poorer. The old people, to help out their income in the hard times after the War, occasionally took in boarders from the neighbouring town, and that spring Michael Bristowe had been sent to them to complete his convalescence after a fresh bout of the lung trouble that had kept him out of the army.

Hilda always went to see the Naylors soon after she arrived home, and on this occasion, naturally, Michael was introduced to her. I gathered that his very "difficultness" (the new noun is necessary) had attracted her, as warm-hearted women are apt to be drawn to shy, awkward young men. She alluded in a manner that I found rather touching to her own recent experience of that expansion, that opening of the heart, the climax of adolescence, which often comes to young people reaching adult life under favourable conditions, frequently in the more intelligent types coming to flower in the congenial atmosphere of the university. For a little while, such a very little while, alas! one feels that the world is really good, that every human being is essentially beautiful, and that one's own capacity for sympathy

is infinite. Hilda hesitated and fumbled a little over her description of this phase, not with any embarrassment, but in the sheer
difficulty of exact expression, until I could do no less than show
that I understood what she meant and could see well enough
how she had come to make friends with young Bristowe.

As for him, his attitude was no less easy to understand. I saw
that the morose thwarted boy, unable to mix comfortably with
his kind (I could sometimes feel sympathy for Bristowe when
he was not there), who would never under any circumstances
have confided in one of his own sex, would have little chance
of resisting Hilda in this mood. Her impulsive sincerity would
sweep aside all his reticences and evasions.

And her friends, the old Naylor couple, had also been frankly
enthusiastic about Michael, in spite of his unsociable traits, for
the old man had already discovered that his guest had the "dowsing" faculty to a high degree. Old Naylor himself was an expert
with the twig, and was consulted whenever it was proposed to
make a new well anywhere in the neighbourhood. He had taken
Michael with him on one of these occasions (which now came
rarely), and had persuaded him to try his hand. After one or
two attempts Michael had thrown the twig away, saying that it
bothered him, and proceeded to dowse very successfully merely
with his extended hands, a method which very few diviners are
capable of using, and then only after long experience.

I interrupted Hilda at this point. "Then it's a thing that can
be improved by practice?"

Hilda, giving me her clear look, said that it undoubtedly
was so, adding, "And that's important too."

The occasional individuals who possess this queer faculty
down in our West Country are always very proud of it and

receive an almost superstitious admiration from their neighbours, in spite of its decreasing practical value. Old Naylor
himself had, as I remembered, a kind of patriarchal dignity due,
I believe, to his consciousness of this distinction. They therefore
made much of Michael when his exceptional gift was known,
and delightedly traced his relationship on his mother's side to a
very famous "dowser" of the district several generations back.

Hilda was only mildly interested, having been familiar with
such things all her life. Nevertheless, she and Michael discussed
it a little, especially one day when she had had tea at the farm
and he was walking back with her in the August evening. He
told her that he had always known from his childhood when
he was passing over water, or rather he had known that there
was something unusual below the ground, though he had never
identified the sensation before his recent experiences.

"Bléton, the French dowser, used to turn giddy," I contrib-
uted a stray scrap of information.

"Well, I can't tell you exactly how it came about," Hilda
went on (I remember this part of the story almost literally, I
think, because, in spite of myself, it impressed me), "but we
began talking about the queer ideas children have, and how
they never tell them; and from that, we passed on to odd sensations generally, and how one can never really know that other
people's experience actually corresponds to one's own. Once
Michael began talking—and it was rather pathetic, Ralph; I
found I had to break the ice afresh every time we met—he was
so eager that it was sometimes difficult to follow him. He began
to talk enthusiastically this time about the 'feeling of things,'
the loveliness of the grass in the country and the pure air, and
the dreadful discordances one felt in the town, and so on. At

first I thought he was being a bit sentimentally poetic—at least, I know that's not a possible description, because one can't be sentimental and poetic at the same time—"

I truly believe that it was at this moment that I began to love Hilda.

"—but, you know, a little high-flown, as young people are apt to be at times. And then, the next moment, he said that of course things were so much fainter under the ground that he quite understood that everyone couldn't distinguish them. But sometimes people behaved so queerly that he had almost begun to wonder whether they really felt anything at all. And then he pulled himself up quickly and said that, of course, that must be all nonsense. Then he looked at me and drew in a breath just like a timid child taking a plunge, and said, 'Of course, you feel that metal thing the other side of the hedge just as much as I do?'"

At the moment, as Hilda described it, they were walking along a path beside a bramble hedge too thick to be seen through, but she was walking next to it and, being tall, was able to glance over it quickly. She saw that just at the point they were passing there was an old discarded bit of a reaper or some farming machine.

"That's not really so very odd," I hastened to say. "Most dowsers can find metal as well as water, and if they can feel them underground, it would be strange if they couldn't feel them above."

"Yes. That's quite true. But I didn't know it then," said Hilda quietly. "I'd only known it in connection with the making of wells… And then, a second later, before I could answer, Michael said: 'There's some animal just ahead of us.' He'd hardly got it out when we put up a big hare from the hedge bottom."

"He might have seen it move," I suggested.

"I don't think he did," Hilda said. "Anyhow, it showed me the truth. I realised all in a flash that Michael actually was different from other people. It wasn't a question of imagination, or egotism, or any vague idea; he really was different in a definite way. He could feel things at a distance without seeing them. For the moment, it frightened me. It seemed such a responsibility to have found it out. You see, he didn't know himself. That is, he didn't know that everyone wasn't the same. He'd evidently had inklings, but he couldn't be sure. And he'd never found anyone he could trust enough to talk to before... Of course, it was no more astonishing really, I suppose, than that any dowser should feel the presence of underground water. But then one was used to that. It was just that this was so new."

I asked, "What did you say?"

"I said nothing for the moment. I was frightened, as I tell you. And the hare's springing up had made an interruption, so that it didn't look as if I were purposely ignoring the question. I think he would have let it pass too, if I had said no more—he was so timid about the whole thing. But if there's one thing I'm sure of in life, it is that one must never be afraid—and, especially, not afraid of this sort of thing—I mean of anything that may extend human experience."

She paused a moment as if for me to make a comment, but I had nothing to say to this. It seemed too large a subject to introduce into a conversation that was already carrying sufficient weight. I merely registered a reflection on the incorrigible tendency of youth to make moral generalisations in all conceivable circumstances. Later, I wished that I had shown this generalisation of Hilda's greater respect.

She went on, however: "And then I realised too that I must
be careful not to frighten Michael. You see, one likes to play
sometimes with the idea of one's own exceptional personality,
but have you ever considered how appalling it would be to discover that one really was abnormal in some important way? I
knew I mustn't give Michael a shock, especially as he was only
just recovering from an illness. And there was no time to think,
unless I was to let the occasion slip altogether.

"So I said as quietly as I could that I thought he probably
felt things more acutely than most people, and that it would
be interesting to test the point sometime. He looked at me a
little curiously, but answered in a lighter sort of way that he'd
thought it must be so. People moved their hands so little, and
he could never understand how they could bear to wear gloves.
He would rather go about in blinkers himself."

I remembered how irritated I had felt at Michael's appearing
without gloves when we were going to interview Rosenheimer
in his Kingsway office. It was not a piece of sheer meaningless
slackness, then, as I had supposed. I still reserved judgment as
to what it really was.

It appeared that the two young people had tried their amazing experiment with complete aplomb the next day, using a
little summerhouse in Hilda's garden. Hilda had thought it all
out during a restless night. Michael was blindfolded carefully,
and then asked to identify the various objects which Hilda put
upon the table some way from him. She said his outstretched
hands, feeling the things, as it were, at a distance, moving a
little all the time like a dog's ears, gave her a queer sensation at
first, though she was used to it now. Later on he told her that
the sensations were not confined to his hands, but that hands

were most useful because one could "move them about quickly
and get different views." But the result of the experiment both
relieved and disappointed her a little. Michael's answers seemed
to be much too accurate for pure chance, but there was nothing
like the alarming exactitude she had half expected. He seemed
to be most fully aware of metallic objects, and always recognised
them, though he could discriminate very little between the various kinds of metals. When the object was wooden he said that
there was nothing there, being apparently unable to distinguish
it from the general effect of the wooden table. A cabbage leaf
he called "a sort of grass"; a stone was "a faint street feeling."
After every trial he insisted on raising the bandage in order to
verify his impression by sight.

"If we do this for long," he said exultantly, "I shall soon know
what all the things are."

The remark startled Hilda out of her returning complacency.
Later, she said, she came to understand how impossible it had
been for a totally untrained and unadmitted sense with no
nomenclature of its own to express itself with any precision.

The present experiment ended when she put a young rabbit
on the table, and Michael immediately snatched off his bandage
exclaiming, "It's alive!" When she protested at his impatience,
he demanded how she could expect him to stay blindfolded
when he felt a live thing there? It wasn't reasonable, unless...

And then he broke off, looking at her oddly, and suggested
that she should now be tested in her turn. There was no choice
then but to tell him the truth. He took it more quietly than
she had anticipated. In fact, she got the impression that he had
actually been better prepared for it than he had let her know.
"Or, I think, perhaps, it was that he knew unconsciously all the

time," she said. "You see, it had been rubbed into him from his childhood that he was different in some way from other people. Other people's behaviour differed from his, naturally, since they did not feel the same things nor in the same way. You know they called him 'the flea' at school, because 'he was so jumpy.'" (Yes, I remembered hearing that—it was one of the things that had most disgusted me with Michael Bristowe.) "And he's always been odd man out in the same way, wherever he went. So I think it was actually a relief to him to have the difference defined at last."

My natural impatience with people who consider themselves "different" broke out. "Good Lord! A man needn't make a fool and an outcast of himself," I said, "merely because he has a slight sensibility of a sort that most people haven't."

"I don't know, Ralph,"—Hilda looked at me consideringly. "The way such things work out is not so simple as you might expect. You will understand better when you have seen more of Michael... Anyhow, he did not seem appalled, as I had been afraid he might, but, if anything, a little triumphant for the moment. And then, all of a sudden, his pleasure seemed to collapse, and he jumped up and came over and said to me, 'And you can't feel anything, then? Even you?'

"I said that of course I could feel things when I touched them, their smoothness and roughness and their temperature, and that one could feel heat and cold at a distance, too.

"He said, 'Yes, but you can't tell what things are really like? One thing is just like another to you unless you see or touch or smell it? You can only tell the moon from the sun by looking? And everything is just the same in the dark? Why, you can't know when someone comes up behind you unless you can hear them! Aren't you frightened? It's awful! It's awful!' He was nearly sobbing.

"I think it really impressed me more than anything else that he was so horribly sorry for me. He has never talked to me like that again. He soon realised how matters were and accepted it. When he had got over it a little, I asked him how it seemed to him, was it like being told that everyone else in the world was blind? He said, 'No, not as bad as that, but something like it.' But we've never tried to discuss it from that point of view since. You see there is no common ground. There has never been any language invented to describe this sensation, and, if there had been, I couldn't understand it."

"Well, and what did you do next?" I asked, as she paused.

"Nothing for a time," she confessed. "I felt nervous about him, and spent as much time as I could with him in the next few days. And he was gentle and almost apologetic in a queer sort of way. You see, he couldn't help feeling his superiority."

I must have made some sort of indignant sound, for she looked at me and repeated, "But it is a superiority, Ralph, a real superiority—to know things in more ways than anyone else can... I was fascinated, and I wanted him to go on trying and practising to improve it, if possible, but he always said, 'What's the use?' I think it was simply the feeling that there was no one to share his experience with. I suppose most of us would lose interest in life if we were put alone on a desert island, knowing for certain that we should never see any other human being again. I think Michael felt isolated like that when he knew that no one else felt things as he did. He told me afterwards that he'd tried to find out quietly if old Naylor was at all conscious of materials in the same way, and he thought he was a little, but very slightly. He always knew when animals were in the room—he is one of those people who can't stand cats—and he always turned if Michael came silently up behind him. But it evidently didn't amount to much. Hidden water and metals he only noticed if he had the hazel rod in his hand. And, though the old man was full of tales about water-diviners, there was evidently no one who had approached Michael's sensitiveness.

"And, then, one day Michael got a letter from home. He showed it to me. It was a horrid letter, Ralph. It was from his stepmother—his father married again, you know. Michael lost his mother before he left school—they seem to have been very fond of each other; he says his father has always disliked him. The letter said they couldn't afford to pay for him at the farm more than another fortnight, and he must go home unless he could find some way of paying his own expenses. It was put about as unpleasantly as such a thing could be put.

"Michael got into a dreadful mood over that (he does have moods, you know), and I tried to help him as well as I could. He said he couldn't go on living at home much longer, but he didn't know what to do, because he had never been trained for any trade or profession, owing to his illness, and there was no money to pay for a training, either. In any case, the conditions for getting work were hopeless, of course, even worse than they are now. All the same, it seemed absurd to me that a person with a power like Michael's should be at a loss in the world, and I said so plainly. He stared at me as if he were slowly waking up and, after a bit, he said, 'You think I might use that? That it might get me out of this?'

"And, after that, I had no need to persuade him to go on trying the thing. He wanted to be at it all the time. He kept saying things like, 'Yes, I'll get on top.' 'I'll show them!' I tried to alter that attitude, but it certainly stimulated him to develop his faculty in the most astonishing way in that fortnight. He learned to make all sorts of new distinctions. He found he could judge distance and direction more or less, but only get vague notions of size and shape. With buried things, he said that it was much more difficult, because they were much fainter and more confused with all the substances that came between, but even at that part of it he was getting much better. Only he couldn't distinguish all the metals from each other."

"As we found the other day," I put in a little grimly.

"Yes... In the first week, he improved in an incredible way. I suppose the faculty had just been waiting, as I imagine one's sight or hearing might have remained in abeyance if one had been born among blind or deaf people. You know how children learn at first—how they have all the colours named to them and the letters and so on, and then are asked, 'What colour is that? What letter is that?' until they get it right. At first, they are apt to call every bright colour 'red,' just as they call every man 'Da-da.' I suppose it was like that when Michael called the cabbage leaf 'grass.' One can't begin to think and make distinctions to any extent until one has learnt the names for one's perceptions. It's like trying to make complicated calculations without pencil and paper. But I suppose he got on so fast because he was already grown up and desperately interested. Afterwards, his progress seemed to slow down. And then the fortnight was up and, soon after, I had to go back to College. He promised that he would go on working alone. We agreed not to talk about it to other people until he was more expert."

Hilda stopped, as if her explanation were complete. But it was far from complete from my point of view.

I have already defined my mental reception of the story. How much of it did I accept and how much did I discredit? The question is unanswerable. Belief and unbelief are uncompromising words. In practice, they are represented by vague, wavering, composite mental states blown about by every wind of prejudice and inclination. As I have said, I never at this time—nor, perhaps, at any time—regarded Bristowe's case from the position of a detached observer, but from my point of view as a man of the world who wanted Hilda Torrington for my wife. It was out of the question to doubt Hilda's sincerity, but I had not at that time, so soon after my long and crucial absence, fully realised the fineness of her intellectual temper. I thought, I was quite ready to think, that she might have exaggerated Michael's odd faculty. Two young people, imagining they have discovered something wonderful—how easy for them to deceive themselves and each other! No doubt, Michael had the dowser's faculty. Well, everyone knew about that. It was just a queer little human aberration of no great significance. Even if they had not exaggerated its increased potency in Michael, Hilda was certainly allowing it to loom too large in her imagination. There was no harm in having amused themselves with it on a holiday. But that did not explain why young Bristowe was now here in London, haunting Hilda's flat, and, as I suspected, sponging on her for other things besides her influence to find him a job. I asked her with careful casualness how he came to be in London now.

It appeared that after Hilda's departure they had corresponded from time to time, but for Hilda the thing soon became overlaid with the interests of her last year at the university, her

Finals and her new work. She had only been back to her home for a few hurried days to collect her belongings. She owned that she had temporarily forgotten Michael. I wished that the oblivion had lasted.

But it was too much, of course, to expect that a "lonely soul" would allow so easy an escape to the person who had been rash enough to become his confidant. A few months back he had written and said he was coming to Town to consult her and look for some means of supporting himself. The birth of a half-sister and subsequent expenses had made his position at home untenable, especially as he was now in good health. His stepmother had become unendurable.

"So, like a young fool," I finished for her, "he flung off here without finding anything to come to first?"

"He wanted chiefly to see me," said Hilda. "To discuss what he was to do. I've explained why I was the only person he could talk it over with. He hasn't got very much farther in the interval, partly because of his home troubles, partly, I'm afraid, because I wasn't there to encourage him."

"Frankly," I said, "I think that a good thing. He would only find it a blind alley. He'd much better set to work and learn something useful."

Hilda looked at me curiously. "Then it doesn't seem at all important to you," she said slowly, "that Michael has the beginnings of a new mode of experience—that he knows what 'things are like,' as he said, in another way than we do?"

"My dear Hilda," I said, "when a man's got his living to earn…"

"Yes, of course. That's what everyone says… No one seems interested. Michael's had an awful time these last few months.

Most of them won't even listen to him, and even the few who have seen what he can do seem to imagine it's a kind of game of thought-transference—a sort of parlour trick, you know. And it's astonishing how everyone sheers off nowadays as soon as you suggest you want employment... But I thought that you might see it differently."

She looked at me a little wistfully. I was sorry; it seemed a pity to prick her little coloured bubble, but I felt that the moment had come to speak trenchantly. It was not until much later that I began to wonder whether, in that wistful glance of Hilda's, it was not, after all, I who was tried by Providence and found wanting.

I said, "You are giving this thing undue importance. What you have told me is very interesting—as a curiosity, that is. But, after all, what does this odd sensibility of Bristowe's amount to? Can it actually do more for him than an ordinary man can do with his eyes? Even if it could penetrate underground with any reliability..."

"I think it might become reliable for that," said Hilda, reflectively, "with more exercise, of course." She drew herself together and spoke more briskly. "But you needn't go on, Ralph. I quite see that, in his own crude way, old Rosenheimer was right. It's clear that Michael's gift is not what they call 'marketable' at present. And we have to take the world as we find it—it's no good attempting to behave as if we lived under ideal conditions." Hilda brought out these truisms as if they were just freshly attained knowledge, as, no doubt, to her, they were. "We must get an ordinary job for him for the time being," she concluded firmly.

I felt greatly encouraged. "That's right. We'll find the lad a job, and then he'll soon settle down... And, after that—look here, Hilda"—the protest did not come well after what had passed, but I was determined that it should be uttered. "The truth is, that Michael Bristowe is not your sort and never will be. Whatever freakish knack he may have about him, the fact remains that he is not your sort. I quite understand how you came to make friends with him in the way you say; but, believe me, it isn't necessary to take up all these youthful friendships again afterwards. In fact, it's a mistake. One can't afford it. The world isn't made that way. If you asked Bristowe to dinner with a number of your real friends, you'd realise in a moment what I meant. He wouldn't fit. Don't think me cynical when I tell you that these 'odd men out' remain 'odd men out' to the end of the chapter. And it's at one's peril that one associates with them. It's infectious. In the long run, you don't even help *them*."

Hilda had listened patiently enough. "I don't think you cynical, Ralph," she said. "No doubt you are right from your point of view. But we see this case differently. You see, I believe that I can help Michael. I believe he is quite a case apart—an 'ugly duckling' and not the usual sort of 'odd man out' at all. And I believe, I can't be sure, but I suspect, that it might be the worst sort of crime one can commit if I did not help him."

"My dear girl, your notions of obligation are fantastic... I am going to take the privilege of an old friend and be even more explicit. Don't you realise that, if you see so much of a young man in Bristowe's position and spend so much time alone with him, as I suppose you will have to if you carry on this absurd 'training,' you may find you have inadvertently committed yourself in another way?"

To my extreme disconcertment Hilda gave a little laugh of pure amusement—and laughter is rare with her.

"Oh, Ralph, and you call that being explicit! I have no intention of marrying Michael, if that is what you mean."

It is not pleasant to have one's delicacies swept aside by the very person they were designed to protect. For the rest of the evening we talked of those neutral topics which I had originally intended should be the staple of our conversation.

I I I

I OWE IT TO MY ANNOYANCE WITH HILDA THAT I SAW NOTH-
ing of the next stage of Michael Bristowe's development.
Sometimes, looking back now, it seems that my behaviour in
keeping away from her after that dinner at the Parthenon was
childish; sometimes, I wish that, childish or no, I had kept up
my resentment and never gone back again at all. However, I
went back.

It was some months later. I had amused myself sufficiently
in the interim. It was several years since I had been in London,
long enough to give it the zest of freshness and not long enough
for my former friends to have forgotten me entirely. Moreover,
I had enhanced my literary reputation in the meantime, so that
everyone was prepared to make things very pleasant for me.
And few things can be pleasanter than London in a fine autumn,
when there is an adequate balance at one's bank and Fortune
is smiling upon one.

Nevertheless, I did not forget Hilda. I thought about her a
good deal from time to time—cursing mentally at her foolish
obstinacy in rejecting the counsel of experience. I thought of
her the more that I was so angry with her.

And then, one morning, I found suddenly that I was thinking about the matter in quite a different spirit. It was one of
those curious mental *volte-faces* which occasionally happen in
matters of sentiment, and are apt to declare themselves quite

suddenly, though, no doubt, they have unconsciously been long preparing. I found that I was seeing Hilda again now as a lonely and pathetic figure in need of my help and protection. After all, I reflected, she was still a child, though an obstinate one, and there was no one to look after her. This business of Michael Bristowe was merely a youthful enthusiasm. I had had opportunities to observe my sister as well as other girl relatives, and I had not gone about with my eyes shut. I knew that girls, as well as boys, had these enthusiasms—about actors, about religion, about socialism, about persons of either sex, about anything in the world that happened to catch their young imaginations. In spite of Hilda's intelligence and logical faculty (which, I faintly began to see even then, might itself come to be a danger in some circumstances), no one who met her could mistake the youthfulness of her temperament. A man of my experience should have known better than to take offence.

I began to feel myself a deserter. Wasn't that, in fact, the whole trouble? I had been away too long. I realised now that some of my anger had been, at bottom, against myself. I had stayed away too long, and had allowed this young girl, whom I had thought of as my probable future wife, to grow up forgetting about me and developing alien interests.

And at this point I discovered that, in spite of what had happened, my intention that Hilda should be my wife was stronger than it had ever been before, and the idea that I might now find it more difficult to carry out than I had expected dismayed me a little.

I sat down after breakfast to think the matter out dispassionately over a pipe. There was no doubt now that I was going back, but I had to consider what line I should take when I got there. I

THE MAN WITH SIX SENSES

decided that I had made a mistake in attacking her relations with Bristowe directly. A high-spirited girl would be sure to resent that. But then Hilda had not resented it, I remembered. She had merely explained to me quietly her reasons for not taking my advice. She was certainly an unusual girl… Nevertheless, it is always the sounder principle in trying to destroy some mental preoccupation to begin by drawing the attention elsewhere. I saw that what I must do was to give her a new and stronger interest, and then young Bristowe would quickly drop back into his proper place in her cosmos. She had given me the hint herself (if I had had the sense to take it), when she said that the interests of her college career had almost made her forget about him during her last year at Cambridge.

It seemed to me that I could not do better than begin at once to introduce to her the interest which I certainly, by this time, hoped would become her strongest. I reflected that there is nothing like a serious love-affair for restoring a girl's sense of proportion. I did not think she would accept my offer immediately, since I felt fairly certain that she had never yet contemplated anything of the sort at close quarters. But it would give her something new to think about—that was the important point.

I know a man of intelligence—a best-seller, in fact, of the cynical variety—who maintains, more or less seriously, the view that the world is run by a Providence who is in reality nothing but a practical joker—a sort of hobbledehoy god, with a crude taste in humour, who has no other idea than to treat his creatures as the clown is treated in a circus. This is not my philosophy any more than Hilda's philosophy is mine. But I must own that it would account well enough for the events of that first evening, the evening when I actually came up against my problem. It was the evening when I proposed to Hilda, it was the evening when I got my first personal intimation of the uncanny quality of Michael Bristowe. Circumstances turned the intimation into the form of a mortifying practical joke against myself. And, at the same time, instead of leading up to my proposal, they led away from it, so that I had finally to make it by a sort of *tour de force*, with the result that it fared as any proposal would be likely to under such conditions.

I found, of course, Michael Bristowe already there when I arrived. He was alone in the little sitting-room, into which I was shown, lying back slackly in an arm-chair before the fire, looking very much at home. On the table were the remains of a meal for two people, which, as I saw at a glance, had been one of those miscellaneous meals usual in Bohemian circles rather than a civilised dinner. This fact immediately disjointed my plans, since I had intended, if I could arrange it, to take Hilda out to dinner. It had not been possible for me to ring her up to make arrangements at the late hour that I had come to my decision, as I did not know her office number or address. At the same time, I had been absurdly unwilling to wait another day. I saw that I should have to pay the penalty of my impatience.

Bristowe did not stir as I came in, but, though his back was half turned to me, I saw an instant tension in his figure like the sudden alertnesses of a dog, so often incomprehensible to his human companions. And, at the same moment, I was conscious of an odd sensation, half repulsion, half an indefinable perturbation at the mere sight of him. I had not felt this on the previous occasions of seeing him, objectionable as his presence had been to me, and I do not know whether it came from the memory of Hilda's queer story, though I had only half accepted it, or whether it was that there had actually been some alteration in the interval. There is no doubt, however, in the light of later knowledge, that, through all this time, the power and range of his special sense, and therefore, I suppose, the degree of his unlikeness to other men, was increasing rapidly.

However, I decided at the moment that my uneasiness was merely the effect of suggestion, and then, as always, did my best to ignore it. I did not want to be unjust to the boy, and it seemed inadmissible to yield to any such intangible influence. At the same time I was impelled to break up his immobile pose, with its uncomfortable hint of suppressed vitality, by speaking and going forward to shake hands. I put cordiality into my tone, too, having decided that a carefully measured friendliness towards him must be a part of my plan of campaign. We had not met since the Rosenheimer fiasco, and I was half prepared for some incivility. But he merely raised himself with a lithe movement, again queerly suggestive of animal-like elasticity, and regarded me with his usual watchful lowering of thick brows.

The ghost of an impudent grin twitched the corners of his lips as he looked at my outstretched hand, but he responded without more than a second's hesitation, and we clasped. Then just as my grasp was falling away, came a sudden increase of consciousness in the contact, and for a few seconds his hand closed firmly on mine. I drew away sharply then, annoyed. I could not imagine why on earth the cub should put this ridiculous warmth into our greeting. Whether it was mere mockery, or a flash of inexplicable sentimentality, it was equally offensive. I glanced at him indignantly. He was settling into his arm-chair, smiling again, as if in secret amusement.

Then Hilda came in, and for the moment I forgot him. Once again, I found that I had idealised her in the interval of absence. I saw now that she was just a tall good-looking girl with golden-brown hair and a fair, clear-featured face. Her russet dress could not by any stretch of politeness have been called an evening gown, though it was fresh and dainty. And then she spoke, and welcomed me with a quiet, frank pleasure and an apparent oblivion of my long defection which was almost insulting; and I knew again at once that, whether there was anything remarkable about her or not, she was the woman I wanted and intended to have.

She asked me if I had dined, casting a deprecating glance at the table, which the small servant-girl, following her in, had begun to clear. I decided in an instantaneous calculation that, if I was to outstay Bristowe and to get my important question put that night, I must be content to postpone my own meal indefinitely.

"Oh yes…" I began, and at the same moment Bristowe's voice sounded behind me:

"No, he hasn't. He's hungry."

I turned and stared at him. "You are mistaken," I said levelly. "I have just come from an early dinner."

Bristowe regarded me with smiling eyes. "I'm very sorry. My mistake," he said suavely, and turned to Hilda with an air of mock humility. "I have not got that right yet, you see, Hilda. And I had his hand, too."

"Never mind, it will come," Hilda smiled at him.

The mystification bothered me. "I don't understand," I said sharply.

"Michael is trying to learn about human beings now," Hilda explained, as she drew out chairs and made me sit down. "They seem to him slightly different at different times, and he's trying to identify the variations. I suppose the chemistry of the body alters a little according to one's physiological state, and we think that must be what he notices."

The explanation staggered me. This seemed a long step from water-divining. It was a most unpleasant suggestion. If Bristowe were capable of acquiring such knowledge about his neighbours, he might be capable of all kinds of other undesirable and intrusive detections. Yet it was, no doubt, a natural development of his alleged power to identify substances at a distance. Some realisation of the meaning and possible ramifications of his queer sensibility reached me for the first time, and, with it, a first touch of the panic which I was to feel again more than once in my intercourse with him.

Fear quickly passes into anger with me. A moment later my mind hardened again. After all, it might so easily have been a guess on Bristowe's part. It was early to have dined. No doubt, he had seen my glance at the table as I came in. Anyhow, nothing would induce me now to confess that he had been right. And nothing should prevent me from carrying through the intention with which I had come, if I had to stay all night in order to do it. I pulled myself together and found that Hilda was talking, and that Bristowe was watching me with an expression of amused comprehension. I plunged quickly into the conversation.

I am afraid it was a hostile instinct that prompted me to begin by asking after Michael's material prospects. I felt certain that the answer would not be a triumphant one.

I was right. If Bristowe was not still one of the "unemployed," he had almost better have been. It appeared that, after numberless attempts, he had lately obtained a job as a clerk in one of the big stores. It was poor work, and poorly paid.

"Though, of course, it's only for the time," said Hilda optimistically, and Bristowe's mouth twitched sardonically.

"We agreed that he must get ordinary work for a short time," Hilda went on, a little uneasily, as it seemed to me, "until he was ready to undertake something better; but I didn't want him to accept anything as tiresome as this. He did it himself in a fit of disgust with employment agencies. They *are* depressing places, you know."

Bristowe stirred fretfully in his chair.

"For God's sake, don't talk about them, Hilda," he broke out. "Talk about convict prisons or workhouse wards or East-End doss-houses, if you must, but don't talk about employment agencies. I'd have taken a job in Hell not to go to any more."

And he went on to talk about them himself, not very amusingly, not very picturesquely, but with such a force of indignant passion that a curious atmosphere of dreariness and dismay in which the heart contracts seemed to fill the room. Life looked like a wedge of sodden suet pudding through which one must eat one's grey way interminably. One's feet seemed to ache, there was a pain behind one's eyes, and weights seemed to be dragging at one's body.

As he talked I remembered a sentence of Hilda's that Michael "feels everything, physical and mental, twice as acutely as the ordinary person." I have the weakness of the literary man, too great responsiveness to suggestion, and I was invaded by all this dingy horror from Bristowe's not very clever description. But I have also the complementary curse of dual consciousness. I was becoming aware at the same time that one of those painful,

ridiculous situations was about to develop, in which one man
tries to outstay another, while the hour gets later and later and
the surface of social civility wears thinner and thinner. It was
not the sort of situation in which I have ever cared to involve
myself, and the youth and gaucherie of my rival would make it
the more humiliating. Nevertheless, my mind had jammed like
a cogged wheel, and I knew that I should have to sit there until
Bristowe decided to remove himself, even though it should be
after midnight and I be fainting for lack of food.

And then I had hardly settled down to the prospect, when
it relieved itself quite simply and naturally. Or rather Hilda
relieved it with complete unself-consciousness. She got up, as
Bristowe finished his diatribe and, resting a hand on his shoulder, looked down at him with affectionate concern. It was time
he went home to bed, she said with gentle firmness. He had to
be at work at nine in the morning. There was also a reference
to "practices" three times a week, about which I was careful
not to enquire further.

Hilda went to mix him what was apparently a regular night-
cap. As I glanced at the boy, I felt a little compunction. Now
that his animation had faded, he was obviously tired to death,
lying back white and slack in his chair. The suggestion of unusual vitality in him only made his appearance of weariness the
more poignant now. I saw that, as one would have expected,
he was taking his desk slavery hard. I ought to have been glad
from my standpoint that he had been put to regular work, but
it was Bristowe's exasperating quality that even in one's own
mind one could never "place" him. Even to me, it seemed a
miserable futility that he should be spending the best of his life
addressing envelopes, or whatever his wretched little business

was. I was sorry for him, even while I cursed mentally at the manner in which his eyes followed Hilda about the room, as if she were his one remaining source of hope and comfort.

I was less sorry a moment later when he saw that I was watching him and the mischief flashed again suddenly over his dark face.

"Bring the biscuits too, Hilda," he directed.

"Michael! You can't be hungry again already." She laughed at him from the sideboard.

"I shan't go happy if I don't see Standring eat a few—especially as I see you are mixing him a drink." Michael chuckled.

"He still thinks he's right, Ralph." Hilda tolerantly brought the biscuit jar.

I compromised to the extent of eating a few biscuits, as I sipped my whisky-and-soda. After all, by whatever means, the detestable youth was right: it would have been unsafe for me to take the whisky without food, and I needed both. I saw Hilda glance at me doubtfully. Helplessly, as if I were reading in a book, I saw the sequence of ideas passing through her limpid mind. I saw the doubt give way to an instant's consideration, followed by a gleam of satisfaction. I knew that she had guessed the truth, and that, more mortifying still, she was more pleased that Bristowe had been right than concerned for my own situation. But, though my dear girl had not enough guile always to be tactful, she was always the soul of courtesy. Her brow cleared again immediately, as she put the little complication behind her.

Bristowe had dropped into lethargy again, and only looked the heavier for his whisky. He let Hilda almost put him into his outdoor clothing and see him down into the street. Apparently,

he lived only a short distance away. And, at last, the field was
clear.

It was perhaps the least propitious moment that one could
have chosen for a proposal of marriage. Bristowe had gone,
but he had left an aura of his presence behind him. There are
people, not always particularly beautiful, witty or admirable
in any way, who are nevertheless the centre of any room they
happen to be in. Michael Bristowe, even apart from any display of his exceptional powers, was one of these; one could
never forget his presence, one could never fully concentrate
attention on anything else while he was there, and, after he
had gone away, time must pass and incidents occur, before
those he had left could find themselves moving in another
current of ideas.

I was not in a normal state of mind, or common-sense would
have made me postpone my attempt. I was fatigued and unfed.
Michael's performance had given me a nervous jar which pride
and interest were forcing me mentally to repudiate. I had the
sense of fighting something malicious and grotesque, and was
irrationally convinced that the only way to fight it was to stick
to my intention in the face of everything. Moreover, I had not
been expecting that my proposal would be accepted for that
time; I merely wished, I was determined, to put the idea before
Hilda without delay, more (as I thought then) for her sake than
for my own.

I cannot, in fact, remember exactly how it happened. I
think I must have struck straight across Hilda's conversation,
which was, of course, about Michael. I must anyhow have been
abrupt, and it was natural that she should not take me very
seriously, perhaps. I found it impossible to be very lover-like.

The psychological winds were too contrary. But I made her see before I had finished that my proposition was genuine and considered. I reminded her of the times of our childhood and early youth, when we had obviously been thrown together and designed for each other by our families, and I told her the truth—that I had never seriously considered the possibility of having anyone but herself for my wife.

She was charmingly grave and sincere when she realised that I was in earnest. I found, a little to my surprise, that she had been quite aware of the intentions of our friends in the old days; but that she had ceased to take them seriously since she had been grown up and gone out into the world. I don't think that she actually said that my absence at that (to her) important period had made it inevitable that I should drop into the background of her thoughts, but I could see well enough that that was the truth of it.

She discussed the question with a detachment that, at least, did away with any fears of a rival that I might have entertained. She did not want to marry at present, though she supposed she might some day. She had no special feeling against it, "if one wanted to." She was keenly interested in her work, although, since it was confidential, she did not talk about it. (I may say that I have never noticed any other young political secretary suffering from similar scruples—Hilda's naïve sense of honour becomes at times almost comic.) Most of her spare time was given at present to Michael's affairs. Altogether, she was enjoying her life of independence in London, and had no desire for the ties of domesticity.

This was sufficiently like what I had expected, though I had certainly imagined in my planning of the morning a conversation with something more of warmth and sentiment in it. However, our coolness had the advantage that I made without difficulty my point that she should keep the possibility of our marrying in mind, and that we should continue to see each other from time to time, so that, as I put it, she might "get to know me thoroughly again, and find out whether I was likely to suit her in the end."

"It's pleasant to know that you want me, Ralph." This was the warmest speech that I got from her, as she gave me her hand and her clear glance at parting.

But, although it cheered me momentarily, a black inexplicable depression fell upon me as I made my way home through the streets. Hilda's complete innocence seemed somehow as menacing as it was beautiful. I had done, in spite of difficulties, what I had intended to do. I had obtained the results I expected and hoped for. And yet, somehow, it was all wrong. The atmosphere was wrong; there was something unreal about the business. I can only be vague about it, even now. I am not "psychic," but this was like a psychic impression. If I must rationalise it, perhaps, after all, it comes down to that one little indigestible fact of the evening—the lurking suppressed consciousness that Michael Bristowe had known that I was hungry by the feeling of my hand.

I V

T HERE BEGAN A STRANGE FEVERISH SPACE OF TIME IN
which nothing seemed to happen according to rule. Even
the minutest element of oddity in life seems capable of causing
unexpected modifications in widening circles, as the slightest
alteration of the angle at the centre may cause a vast difference at the circumference. In this case, the centre was Michael
Bristowe's personality with its small divergence. Everything in
his neighbourhood seemed to be affected with slight unpredict-
able variations. My own course obeyed the pull whether I would
or no. I see it like that now; at the time, I merely struggled with
an uncomprehended bafflement.

I saw a great deal of Hilda because I could not keep away
from her. Even when I had made my proposal, I had not
imagined that I was passionately in love with her; nor, looking
back now, does it seem as if, at that point, I had been so. I have
suffered emotions far more intense on other occasions. But the
situation worried me, and I could not leave it alone. Nothing
moved in my affair, I could find no sign in Hilda either of
increased interest in myself, or of diminished interest in Michael
Bristowe. I had chosen to be left in this anomalous position,
and I could not grumble, but I had certainly not calculated
on the consequences of continued suspense for myself. The
truth was that experience had left me without guidance in this
instance, for I had never before had to do with any woman so

little sex-conscious as Hilda. She treated me as an old friend
with whom a possible future business arrangement had been
left temporarily in abeyance. And I had to acquiesce. But I could
not keep away.

During this time I did my best to keep up the attitude I had
deliberately adopted; but occasionally, in spite of myself, my
impatience broke through. I remember one evening, one of the
rare occasions when we were alone together, attacking the work
which she had made her chief pretext for remaining unmarried.

"You can't like working for Mrs. Hastings," I urged. "Women
always bully women. Everyone knows that."

Hilda smiled. "Some do and some don't," she said. "Just like
men… Mrs. Hastings is very pleasant to work for."

I went away in impotent rage against the rational woman
and all her works. I felt sometimes that if I could only get Hilda
to waver in her poise for a moment, to say something thoroughly irrational and unjust, to lose her temper, there might
have been a chance for me to make progress. But she never
did. More than once I asked myself how I could continue to be
interested in such a woman. But every time I went back. She
was young, and she was Hilda, and, whether she knew it yet or
not, she was mine. So my mind moved at that time.

Seeing so much of Hilda, I saw much of Bristowe, also. I had
to accept him as a condition, a *sine qua non*, of Hilda. I got used
to him. I even got used to his peculiarities up to a point, something in the same way as an oyster gets used to a grain of sand
by fencing it off as smoothly as possible. But I did not escape
the nervous strain inherent in such a policy, more especially as
the subject I was trying to avoid was just the subject that was
of supreme interest to my companions. A close association

with people whose view of the relative importance of things is different from one's own, is always difficult. An intimate and involved association with them, such as this, makes one's whole life a harassing problem.

In this respect also, Hilda gave me no help whatever. She did not seem even to perceive that I needed it. It seemed to me that she must have forgotten that first conversation of ours about Michael Bristowe. She talked to me about him at length, she obviously relied on my unbiased interest and help in her plans for him. It seemed as if she saw that I had made up my mind to accept him, and at once put out of her memory my formerly displayed antagonism. I was making a difficult effort about Michael for her sake, but I got no credit for my effort from Hilda. I suppose that temperaments still incapable of love are also incapable of understanding love's egotism. And Michael and his gift were so intensely interesting to her that they obliterated such smaller considerations as any prejudice of mine. That I still "funked" Michael Bristowe was certainly no fault of Hilda's, who has never funked anything in her life.

For I fear that "funk" is the true description of my attitude. I funked him as one may begin to funk an acquaintance who shows signs of becoming a criminal or a lunatic, or of developing some loathsome disease. I thought about him and his peculiarity and his affairs as little as I possibly could. I do not like oddities. And I could no longer conceal from myself that he was definitely an oddity. I even feared secretly that, as Hilda thought, he might be a momentous sort of oddity, though this I would never admit even to myself. In spite of Hilda, I avoided witnessing any systematic demonstrations of his power; yet I was always coming up against little differences, odd scraps of knowledge and intuition in him, which disturbed me more than I would acknowledge.

There was the evening when Hilda made him detect a new cigarette-case in my pocket from several yards' distance. I never liked to see his moving, groping, hesitating fingers, as it were, pick up the scent.

"Gold," he said, promptly. "A little alloyed. Not badly."

"Yes?" Hilda looked at him smiling.

"All right. I'll try." The two talked in the elliptical speech which people on very intimate terms are apt to develop.

Michael turned back to me with a frown of concentration, his hands stretched in my direction, his eyes half closed. I felt a slight shiver pass over me, as I waited. To see a human being adopting an inexplicable attitude obviously relating to oneself seems to arouse some old primitive fear from the time when it was a matter of life and death to watch the movements of the living beings around one.

Michael stood for some time, while I held myself rigid. After a moment, I was astonished to notice the sweat break out on his forehead.

"18-carat," he burst out suddenly at last. And then, sitting down, buried his face in his hands.

Hilda went over to him quickly, and slipped an arm round his shoulders. "I wonder why that's so difficult, Michael?"

He looked up with an hysterical laugh. "Oh, I can't explain that to you... And I didn't do it, after all. How could old Standring have anything that wasn't 18-carat?... As soon as I thought of that, it was no good going on."

He was quiet after that, and there was no mistaking the effect of strain. I wondered in a bewildered despair where all this was to end. It seemed not only queer, but somehow irrelevant to the world I knew. The rules did not cover it.

It must have been one of these evenings also that I first noticed the ridiculous business of the sugar. Hilda always put the bowl out on the sideboard when she was expecting Bristowe.

"He loves the crystals," she explained when I remarked upon it.

The absurdity of this broke down my habit of ignoring Michael's peculiarities as far as I could. I said something sarcastic about "preposterous fads and fancies."

Hilda knitted her brow in the effort of interpretation. "You see, for Michael, his faculty isn't a question of being able to do odd stunts as it is to the rest of us. It's a question of living in a different sort of world all the time. Besides all the sensations we get from everything round about—shapes, colours, sounds, scents—he gets a whole class of other sensations as well, which he feels in a way we can't even begin to understand. Try to imagine yourself describing what things look like to a man born blind and you'll see how poor Michael is placed with regard to the rest of us. And, of course, this becomes more and more marked as his sense gets finer and keener. He told me that a bowl of sugar crystals placed openly on the sideboard affected him like a bowl of daffodils in the room. He loves crystals and hates confused substances."

"A bowl of daffodils!" In spite of myself, a preposterous vision of the world idealised for a race of Michael Bristowes flashed across my mind—parks with beds of crystals arranged in unknown harmonious combinations, knobs of spar carried in one's buttonhole—it was on the cards even, that a seaside pebble would be more beautiful to him than the Koh-i-noor. For a second my imagination tried to plunge further and to obtain some more comprehensive notion of what the world might seem like to Michael Bristowe, if it were indeed with him as Hilda supposed; but I experienced the immediate intellectual blockage which I had felt as a lad when the algebra master had handled so glibly the odd symbols of infinity and nothingness, or that impossible quantity (absurdly called "imaginary," since it is unimaginable), the square root of minus one, by means of which so many formulæ are obtained and so many problems solved. I had never been happy in the use of these symbols because they symbolised no reality, but a swimming brain had taught me not to question them. Now, as then, it seemed that the flaming sword that protects the tree of abstruse knowledge waved threateningly before me, as I tried to think myself into the skin of Michael Bristowe.

I wondered how Hilda herself carried the burden of her close association with him if she really thought of him like that. She must, I supposed, be more like the algebra master, have more of the scientific spirit than I, and be content to manœuvre with things without knowing what they were. It was, of course, the only sane way of regarding Bristowe, if one must regard him at all. Only by studying results was it possible to learn anything of him and his unplumbed capacities.

Yet the fantastic practicality of that bowl of sugar on the sideboard moved me to irritated amusement. If Michael was indeed acted upon incessantly by such vast numbers and combinations of influences from the substances around him, the little sugar-basin seemed too wildly inadequate to the situation to be anything but laughable—a gallant and pathetic symbol of Hilda's resolution to cope, as she could, with the unknown.

Having begun to think, I found it impossible to stop. Coming to matters more practical—back, in fact, to the crux of my problem—I began to wonder how Bristowe himself was seeing Hilda and me and the whole position. But this line of thought was no less baffling than the other. Here, too, that incalculable factor in him defied all analysis. I don't know how he thought or how he felt. To an outside observer, although they were nearly of an age, his relation to Hilda was like that of a wilful, but dependent, son to a young mother. I saw well enough that, as Hilda had said, I had no occasion for jealousy in the narrow sense. Michael obviously wanted her, her care of him, her faith and solicitude. She was the only human being who really believed in and encouraged him—I cannot say, understood him, since it was, I suppose, the pathos of his position that it was impossible that anyone should understand him. But his want was far from the want of sexual desire. He wanted her for a purpose, to help him to develop this queer difference in him which was actually the root of all his troubles, but, at the same time, his only claim to distinction.

At this point Bristowe himself came in and interrupted us. We both looked at him anxiously, and relaxed again as he made a sufficiently cheerful remark and threw himself into his usual chair. It infuriated me to see how sensitive we were becoming to his moods—myself as well as Hilda, by reason of my dependence upon her. I have seen a family react in the same manner to an uncertain-tempered domineering head. Not that Bristowe, to do him justice, was actually a bully. It was just his quality of absorbing attention, and it was the more nerve-racking in that his moods were influenced by things imperceptible to us. Sometimes there would be a smile of delight at some harmony for which we had no recognition. More often it would be a nervous start or a frown. I understood by this time why they had called him after the jumping creature at school.

There came a Saturday that I went there to tea and found Bristowe pacing up and down the little sitting-room like a caged animal, his face flushed and his eyes shining, while Hilda regarded him, smiling a little watchfully, from a chair. It was a wild mood which I had never seen before. Michael sat down and got up again, laughed at nothing, made atrocious puns in every other sentence. He was like a child crazy with excitement, and could not keep still for two minutes together. The little room was not large enough for his restlessness, and I expected every moment to see a chair knocked over, or a plate of biscuits flying. Another man could hardly have avoided some such mishap if he had behaved in the same manner; but with Michael, some slight supple evasion always saved the position at the last moment. It was another of his peculiarities. There was always this smooth pliancy in his movements. His muscles seemed to work softly, like a cat's, and with the same instantaneous adjustment. Hilda, I remember, thought that this trait must be due to the perpetual tense consciousness of physical nerves which one must suppose that he possessed.

All this time he was talking to Hilda in short allusive phrases, as he often did, disregarding my presence with a complete lack of ordinary courtesy. It was one of the most trying of the small irritations that I had to endure that Hilda never made any attempt to check him in this habit. As usual, I could not make out what they were talking about, and, to cover my mortification, I picked up a book from a pile that was lying on a small table.

The innocent action had immediate absurd results. Michael stopped in the middle of a boisterous laugh, strode over and addressed me in a sharp dictatorial voice, as if I were attempting to thwart him in some unreasonable manner.

"Here, please, Standring, I want that." And he took the book out of my hand without further ceremony. I had barely had time to notice more than that it was a work on Electricity and Magnetism. He turned on Hilda. "I've got to read these books at once. What have you been keeping me for?" He gathered the pile under his arm, glancing again distrustfully at me, as if he suspected me of wanting to take them from him.

"Well, I won't keep you any longer"—Hilda accepted the utterly unwarranted accusation with an unperturbed smile— "though you haven't had much tea. Here's a bun to put in your pocket."

Bristowe caught the bun as he went through the door, turned a grinning face, pleased at his own adroitness, upon us for a second, crammed his cap on his head and vanished.

The room felt like a lull in a gale at sea.

"What in the world is the matter?" I was too much shaken up to remember my policy of ignoring Michael and his vagaries.

Hilda was leaning back in her chair, also relaxing after the tempest. "Partly, I think, that a thunderstorm is coming," she said, glancing at the window, from which we could see a black accumulating mountain of cloud over the opposite chimney-pots. "They always excite Michael... But more what we have been doing this afternoon."

I had not seen her for a day or two previously. It was early summer, my sister was in Town, and uncontrollably filling up my time with engagements. Hilda's latest movements in Bristowe's interests had, therefore, escaped me; but I had noticed a name that did not reassure me on the flyleaf of the book that I had picked up, and had heard the same name thrown about in their fragmentary conversation.

"You've been seeing Henry Selver?" I said.

Hilda assented. "I heard that he had a private laboratory, so I got someone I know to introduce us. We were trying Michael with magnets and magnetised substances. Apparently, they are much more vivid to him than when they are unmagnetised."

I asked for Selver's views, reserving my misgivings.

"He was interested," she told me. "He said it didn't appear to be precisely a question of magnetic force, though it obviously had to do with the architectural structure of matter, like magnetism. He said that it wasn't the first time something of the sort had been heard of."

Curiosity drove me to further questions.

It seemed that there had been a German scientist called Von Reichenbach, about the middle of last century, who claimed to have discovered a new sense in human beings; but, as all his best subjects appeared to be invalid girls, no one had taken him very seriously. He had begun by magnetic and electricity tests, but found that they did not cover the facts.

Selver had said that the same thing was true of water-diviners. Sometimes the faculty could be blocked by insulating the dowser, sometimes not. No one understood why... If Von Reichenbach could be trusted, after all, his best subject had had the sense in a higher degree than Michael; though she always expressed the sensation in terms of heat and cold, even when it involved saying that sunlight was cold.

"Michael laughed at that," Hilda told me. "He said, 'I suppose one might think of it that way!'... He got excited, especially over the magnets—too excited, as you saw. I had hard work to get him away."

I reflected a moment. The news was partly welcome, partly not. Selver's views were vaguely reassuring. They made Michael less of a freak. The thing had been heard of before. It was connected with magnetism. This seemed to make it safer and saner in some way. I knew in my heart that the fact did not really make it any the less marvellous. Yet it is strange how the mere naming of a thing comforts a man. It makes generalisation possible—that eternal refuge of shivering minds. It enables one to drug oneself with the delusion that one really understands.

At the same time, the appearance of Henry Selver himself in this galley disturbed me. I knew something of him—he was a scientific dabbler, who often wrote popular "scientific" articles for the Press. I had no very high opinion of him. I like a man to be either a writer or a scientist. A man who stands half-way between two professions is very apt, as they say of half-breeds, to inherit the worst from both sides.

I asked Hilda whether she supposed he was likely to be of any use to them.

"He said he might be able to do something later by calling attention to Michael in the Press," she told me. "Just at present it seems to be a bad moment, because there is so much news of strikes and other things, that no one would be likely to take much notice if he introduced it. Meanwhile, we had better go on experimenting, he said."

I smiled grimly to myself. I saw Selver's idea as if I had been inside him. He would watch and study the thing a bit, and then, if it seemed sufficiently promising, he would choose his moment, and start one of those journalistic stunts which in his soul he loved—even apart from the fact that they paid for his winters on the Riviera. It might, or might not, be of service to Michael. The minute it was played out, in the journalistic sense, Selver would drop it without a second's hesitation and be off in the Blue Train with bulging pockets. I began to question Hilda tentatively, and discovered, to my relief, that she was not really imposed upon by his shop-window manners.

But she added, frowning a little, "We must take what help we can get, Ralph. I am beginning to be bothered about Michael. His fits of depression are getting worse. I don't think he will stand his job at Harding's much longer. He's had nearly six months of it now, you know."

"Michael is neurotic," I said. "He can't stand what other people seem able to stand perfectly well."

I could not prevent my growing exasperation with the whole position from venting itself occasionally in such remarks as this, though I knew well enough that they would only bring upon me Hilda's patient attempts to give me a better understanding of Michael. It was so now.

"I don't think he's neurotic by nature, Ralph." But the words came slowly to-day, and I did not like to see the little double wrinkle of worry on her smooth forehead. "What ordinary people like us don't understand is the strain of being exceptional in any way. That strain has been on Michael all his life. People like that become neurotic through sheer collective suggestion unless their exceptional quality is admitted and allowed for. You must remember how it's happened to dozens of poets and artists and musicians. And we shall never know how many geniuses have gone under altogether because of it. It takes an intellectual Titan to stand up under a weight like that. And Michael is not that."

"No," I agreed. The impulse was upon me again to add something disparaging about Michael's intelligence, but I suppressed it with some inward shame. That aspersion would not even have been true. The boy was not stupid, though only half-educated. He had intelligence, even apart from that intangible exasperating superiority of his, that suggestion of experience upon another plane.

"And that," Hilda went on, "is why I am so anxious to get him an established position of some sort, even apart from the money... He needs it to give him confidence. He can't afford to be derelict. He can afford it less than anybody."

I could only agree with her, without seeing any possible way out of the dilemma. So far as Michael's case was capable of diagnosis, no doubt she had diagnosed it. Sometimes, when he had not startled me for awhile, I thought I understood Michael well enough. He was the man who had grown up with what it is the fashion to call an "inferiority complex." This accounted for much in him—for his moodiness, his gaucherie, his rebelliousness, his frequent impertinences. And then again something inexplicable would flash out, a gleam from the other plane on which Hilda said he lived, not only odd bits of information which he could not have obtained by normal means, but more than that, sudden magnanimities, assumptions springing from startling depths of understanding, unexpected indifferences. I suppose that all our boasted knowledge and apprehension is built up, after all, from the material provided by our five senses. We abuse them often enough for deceiving us; yet, apart from them, we have no possibilities. At any rate, it is impossible to imagine a man deaf, blind and anæsthetic from birth as thinking at all, whatever his innate potentialities. Bristowe, on the other hand, had a sixth gateway of knowledge besides those open to other men. He had this together with a human brain to make use of it. After all, animals also have senses of which we know nothing. There is the pigeon's sense of direction, the sense which also presumably directs migrating birds; insects have certainly some, and may have many, senses which we do not possess; a dog's sense of smell is so much keener than ours as to be almost another thing. And yet these creatures are not our masters. It was its conjunction with a man's brain that gave Michael's faculty its significance. He knew more about the world, more about the nature of things, than any seer, poet or philosopher who ever lived. One must suppose that he had strange enlightenments, inconceivable expansions of thought, dependent upon this unique physical possibility of his. They were not transmissible to us who were near him, and only now and then did we catch a glimpse of the exasperating unknown X of the equation we should never solve.

"Michael is so much more important than we are."

This was another sentence of Hilda's, uttered with innocent bluntness, which struck me like the slash of a whip across the face. I see now that half the sting was in my inward misgiving that the statement might be nothing less than the flat truth.

V

B RISTOWE LEFT HIS JOB AT HARDING'S SHORTLY AFTER MY
conversation with Hilda about Henry Selver. I don't think
I ever quite made out whether he had thrown it up of his own
accord, or had been dismissed by the firm. It had appeared so
certain that it must come to an end before long, that the exact
manner of the termination seemed immaterial. Hilda, I remember, attributed it to the fact that an instalment of Michael's
tiny income (he drew about £40 a year from the estate of his
maternal grandfather) had just been paid over to him, and that,
like an improvident poet, he thought it was going to last for
ever and behaved recklessly.

I made some remark about having supposed that that sort
of Bohemian imbecility was out of date. But Hilda merely
replied seriously, as if she were referring to initiation into the
Mysteries:

"You've never been hard up, Ralph."

I did not pursue the subject. I was restless that day, and
almost quarrelled with Hilda because she would not come to
a week-end literary gathering at my sister's Hampshire cottage,
where there were to be people whom I wanted her to meet. I did
not like to see how completely she was dropping out of social
life, and I knew also that her reason for refusing to come was
that Bristowe was coming to her flat every day for his evening
meal. I foresaw that he would soon be living on her altogether.

I wanted to force an issue that evening, but dared not. I was afraid of a real quarrel and a breach, even if only a temporary one; for, by this time, it had become impossible for me to contemplate a stretch of even two days together without seeing Hilda. I had to submit with as good a grace as I could muster.

And then, with the cruel unconscious advantage of the one who does not care, she carried the war into my country and, before I left, I had promised that I would go with her and Michael on their next Sunday expedition into the country. They always went on fine Sundays, and I had been asked to join them more than once, but had always refused hitherto. I understood that she wanted me to see Michael at work in the open country, and it was still my policy, half deliberate, half instinctive, to avoid such occasions. But both my patience and my determination were wearing out in these hot, dusty dregs of a trying summer, during which my obsession had kept me wretchedly and unnecessarily in Town while most of my acquaintances were off to the relief of sea or moors. I made up my mind that I would go this one expedition with them, as I had promised, and that afterwards, at all costs, I would have an explanation with Hilda and force some sort of change in the intolerable situation.

The expedition began more pleasantly than I had expected. We drove out early in the day in order to get ahead of the crowds that overrun the Home Counties like a swarm of locusts on Sunday afternoons in summer. Thus we came early to the country of commons and woods and tasted their exquisite freshness after the dead air of London. We garaged the car and set off across country. Hilda and I had fallen into one of those rare conversations which I so much enjoyed, and the memory of which always reassured me when I was losing all hope and confidence. There are so few people to whom things of the intellect have any real life or attraction. The eager freshness of Hilda's young mind was always a joy and a stimulus to me. On these occasions it seemed to me tragically wasteful that all that fine energy, apart from what she gave to her work, should be spent on Michael Bristowe and his anomalous problem.

That morning's discussion had begun in the car as we ran out, and was concerned with a very provocative and interesting play which had just been produced. It continued while we set off on our walk across the common, and I was pleased to see that Hilda, in her absorption, was hardly noticing Michael, who had taken no share in the conversation and had fallen a little behind us.

Our path took us presently into a little plantation of pines. As we got over the stile at the entrance to the wood, I noticed superficially a man who was standing near-by in the obscurity of the hedge, so that one did not see him until one was right upon him. I was intent on the conversation, and received an impression only vaguely disagreeable. He was a squarely built man, with a hard face, dressed in obviously cheap ready-made clothes. He looked us over closely, yet in a cool impersonal way, as we passed, and such are the queer complications of a civilised man's consciousness that I can truly say that I hardly noticed him, and that, at the same time, my spine tingled at that look of his.

We came through the little plantation and out on to the open heath, a heartening stretch in the early sunshine, and almost deserted except for two men walking some distance away on our right and another solitary figure on the horizon.

Michael was still walking apart from us, or rather ranging lightly to and fro around our track. Hilda now paused to glance at him from time to time. His movements suggested to me nothing so much as a questing hound. He was intent and smiling, obviously happy to be in the open, but he made me uncomfortable in a way exceeding anything his indoor behaviour had ever effected. There was a suggestion of some odd, unclassified animal in his gait; the light and sensitive movements of his long hands, responsive to invisible stimuli, reminded me uncannily of a hind's ears questioning the air. I thought that anyone seeing us would inevitably take him for some unusual kind of lunatic, and was thankful for the comparative desertion of the heath.

It was almost a relief, though I resented the interruptions, that he called sometimes to Hilda in a brief business-like manner such phrases as "Water here!" with sometimes an attempt to estimate depth and direction.

My uneasiness finally compelled me to make a break in the conversation myself, and allude to the matter in an awkward, jesting way:

"Do you think he's going to spot a gold mine?"

"Hardly," Hilda smiled. "There are no metals of any kind around here, I believe. But it's a geological formation that interests Michael for some reason. He says there are some fascinating bits here and there."

We came down off the common presently into a small valley with a stream running down it amid a few low trees and bushes. Hilda and I moved towards a spot where the stream narrowed sufficiently for us to step across it: we could hear Michael, who had wandered off, making his way after us obliquely through the bushes. As I was about to stride across after Hilda the rustle of his near approach stopped suddenly. It was so abrupt that I hesitated for a moment and listened. There was absolute silence. Then, from the bushes a few yards behind, came a kind of whimper, and a moment later a panic-stricken call, "Hilda! Hilda!"

Hilda sprang back across the stream, and, pushing me aside, disappeared into the bushes. I followed her quickly. In a little open space among the undergrowth, Michael, white and shaking, was clinging to her hysterically and chattering brokenly, like a child.

"It's wrong. I tell you it's all wrong. There's something bad."

"Michael, Michael, what's the matter?" Her strong young arm seemed to be all that kept him from collapsing.

There was nothing to be seen.

"Pull yourself together, man." I spoke harshly. I had seen unseasoned youngsters occasionally behave like this the first time they were under fire.

Michael took no notice of me. His eyes were turned to the ground under our feet with a sort of appalled fascination.

"What is it, Michael?" Hilda said again. Even at that moment of perplexity the urgent tenderness of her voice cost me a pang.

"Yes. We'd like to know what it is," a gruff voice broke in suddenly. A big man, followed by a companion, pushed his way into the open beside us. "This young chap seems to be a bit upset." He regarded Michael critically.

"What is it, Michael?" Hilda repeated, taking no notice of the new-comers.

He answered in a half whisper. "I don't know. How can I know? It's the churchyard feel... Something like it, only worse."

The big man had moved forward to listen. As I looked at his hard watchful face I recalled the man we had seen in the upper wood. This was not the same, but there seemed to be a sort of family likeness. He regarded Michael curiously again, and then sent a hurried glance over the surroundings.

"The churchyard feel, is it?" he repeated slowly. "And you 'don't know'?"

"I don't know." Michael drew back. His face was green with nausea.

The big man, not taking his eyes off Michael, muttered a few words to his companion, who had stepped up beside him. The other turned sharply and disappeared up the slope.

"When were you here last?" The stranger stepped up to Michael and fired the question at him abruptly.

"I've never been here before… Oh, let's get away." Michael seized Hilda's arm, and began to drag at her in a desperate manner. "I can't bear it. It's horrible."

"Pardon me," the big man spoke authoritatively. "I must ask you to wait a few moments."

Michael paused and half turned, staring at him slackly with dull eyes. I saw that he was going to faint, and moved over just in time to help Hilda ease down his sagging body. We laid him at length and loosened his tie and collar. I went and soaked my handkerchief in the stream and brought it back dripping. Then, seeing that he was coming round at once, I left him to Hilda and turned back to the stranger. By this time, I was anxious to know more of him.

"You gave orders to my friend rather abruptly. May I ask…?" I finished my words trimly, putting into my tone a certain quality which is one of the few valuable things one learns at a public school.

It worked instantly, confirming the surmise that I had already formed. The man hastily pulled a card from his pocket and handed it to me, muttering an apology. "Sorry, sir. There's been something a bit wrong down this way, and we're obliged… Shan't bother you long."

I saw, as I had expected, that it was a question of Scotland Yard, and a moment later several men pushed their way through the bushes and joined us.

The inspector looked doubtfully across at Michael. He was sitting up now, but still completely demoralised, imploring Hilda to take him away.

After a moment the inspector made up his mind and turned to me. "If you could stay and give me a few particulars, sir, I could send one of my men to help the young lady get your friend home. We've got a car in the road over there—I can lend you that. Otherwise, I'm afraid I should have to keep the lot of you for a bit."

I agreed, and went to put it to Hilda. I can truly say that I know no one else, man or woman, who would have accepted the necessities of the case in such a situation with so few words. I told her I did not myself understand what was the matter, and promised to follow her back to Michael's rooms as soon as I could. They would go in the police car, and I would follow in my own. I warned her that I did not think the detective would leave them for the present.

One of the plain-clothes men, with the assistance of a comrade, got Michael across his shoulders in the "fireman's lift," and strode away with him. Hilda followed behind. The inspector, having given some directions to his subordinates, drew me to one side. He wanted, of course, to know what had "alarmed my friend."

I told him that he knew as well as I did, and got a very

sceptical glance in reply. It took me, in fact, some time to convince him that I was really in the dark even about the bearing of his own questions. I was proceeding to ask questions in my turn, when one of the plain-clothes men stepped up beside us. As we talked, they had been making a minute examination of the little clearing.

"Ground seems to have been disturbed over there, sir," he said.

"Ah? Well, get the spades and we'll see."

I began to understand. But there is, after all, no need to dwell now upon the details of that most unpleasant hour, or on what immediately followed.

V I

THE CRIME THAT WAS DISCOVERED BY MICHAEL BRISTOWE'S agency was a sordid one, of the kind that occupy long columns in the popular Sunday papers, the kind that make a principal topic of conversation for about a week and are forgotten within a month. The police worried Michael a good deal, and it was fortunate for him that he was able to show a complete alibi at all important times. Police officials are not chosen for their imaginative gifts, and it was perhaps natural that they should regard with suspicion a young man who becomes hysterical over the spot where the body of a murdered woman is subsequently disinterred. If there had been the remotest connection of any other kind between him and the victim, he would certainly have been arrested, in spite of the carefully naturalistic account of the capacities of water-diviners that I gave to the inspector.

Bristowe was obliged, of course, to give evidence at the inquest, and there the solicitor whom we employed on his behalf succeeded in getting the admission that no suspicion attached to him.

At this point, I come, I suppose, to a new phase in Michael Bristowe's history, if it were Bristowe's history that I were writing (as, in Hilda's view, it should be) and not rather its reactions upon myself. This is the phase of his opportunity. It must be considered his opportunity, I suppose. At least, most people would consider it so; for the modern world put at his disposal

its greatest and most highly esteemed gift—the chance of publicity. It was as an opportunity that Hilda also saw it as soon as
she had got over the shock of its unpalatable occasion. If she
over-valued it, or put a mistaken value upon it, that was the
fault of her inexperience, the usual tragic fault of young intelligence—that it expects the world to be as intelligent as itself.

Looking back, I see that it was that village coroner who
started the trouble. I recognised him at once spiritually, that
is, I recognised his type, the first moment that he opened his
mouth in court, though no intuition warned me of his capacity
for mischief in this instance. He was a darkish, bearded, middle-
aged man with very bright eyes—one of those not uncommon
unfortunates isolated in provincial surroundings, just clever
enough to be kings of their company with all the damage that
entails, having imagination and ambition out of all proportion
to their opportunities for culture.

His position as coroner must have been one of his few
outlets, and the present notorious inquest gave him what he
must have regarded as the opportunity of a lifetime. The room
was crowded to the doors both with the Londoners who make
these matters their hobby and with local people. There were
strangers to impress and neighbours to see his glory. His questions to Michael involved a subtle self-advertisement.

"How did it happen that you stopped at the point where
the police found you?"

Michael, very pale and slack—he had had to be treated for
shock and was hardly yet recovered—throwing glances of sullen
distaste at the crowded benches, answered with obvious effort.

"I felt something wrong. I could feel something horrible in
the ground... I cannot make it any plainer."

"You felt something? How did you feel it?"

Michael's troubled eyes in his white face turned instinctively to the front bench where Hilda sat beside me; he knew well enough by this time the hopelessness of trying to communicate his unique sensations to his fellow-men. But Hilda could not interpret for him here. I felt her stir responsively, and then relax again with a sigh.

"Come, Mr. Bristowe"—the coroner evidently had enough sensitiveness to receive an inkling of the psychological situation—"it is our duty to get at the truth of this matter as far as we can, you know. We don't wish to try you too far after your illness. But you must give us what help you can... Just give Mr. Bristowe a chair." He was very much master of the situation, and evidently prepared to stretch to its limits the informality of a coroner's court.

Michael looked at him sombrely. "It is a kind of feeling," he said hesitatingly. "I don't know how to explain it. Like another kind of sight, I suppose. It was horrible. It made me feel ill."

"A vague suggestion of horror came over you? Would that express it?"

"No. Not vague at all." Michael's black brows knit suddenly into the familiar scowl. "Nothing could be more distinct. It's a real sensation—chiefly in one's hands and forehead."

The coroner frowned in his turn, and glanced aside, turning over the papers on his table.

"Are you," he enquired, looking up again after a moment, "what is known as 'psychic'?"

And with that word the mischief was done. It did not matter what Michael answered—I think he said sardonically that "he had never seen a ghost," or something of that sort. But the coroner did not question him much further. From his point of view it must have seemed unprofitable. One of the jury, though he did not succeed in making himself very clear, evidently had some notion that if Michael had known so much, he might just as well have known a little more and told them the name of the murderer. But the coroner did not encourage anyone's questions but his own. Michael's answers were not helping him, and the witness's obvious physical weakness gave him his excuse to cut the examination short. The star turn of this piece was to be the summing-up. If my memory serves me, he found himself able to introduce, among other topics, the Einstein Theory, God's Providence, Sir Oliver Lodge, and the present state of Russia. I am sure that he concluded, "There are more things in heaven and earth, Horatio, than are dreamt of in your philosophy."

I can see now the importance of that word "psychic." We were never afterwards able to escape it. The reporters who interviewed us later had been deeply impressed by the coroner's remarks. The coroner's mental calibre was just so much above the average man as the average man can comfortably contemplate. This makes good journalism, and the reporters recognised their provender with a cat's instinct for fish. This stuff was ideal: it was exactly what their public wanted and could digest.

The "million-sale" paper came out next day with the headline, "Clairvoyant Discovers Murder," and the others followed similar lines. The statements made by Michael and Hilda (I myself declined to be interviewed) were dexterously turned to bear out the theses of the writers. It was a bewildering turn of the wheel. In a night Michael had become famous; and, at

the same time, he had become completely commonplace. He
was labelled. He was a "clairvoyant."

I was against publicity from the start, partly from a general
dislike for journalistic blatancy, partly from my knowledge of
the realities of journalism. Hilda, on the other hand, had made
up her mind that, in however odd a guise, this was Michael's
chance, and that he must not miss it. It was in vain that I pointed
out the probable pitfalls.

"We can't help it, Ralph," she said. "I feel that people ought
to know about Michael. He is too important to keep to ourselves. If they can't make anything of him, that won't be our
fault. We shall have given them the chance."

It both grieved and tickled me in the following days to see
my poor girl trying to make headway against what the Press
and the public had decided to believe. I even relented and helped
her a little, and told her and Michael the most hopeful methods
to employ, so that we succeeded before the week was out in
getting a more realistic headline, "Is There a Sixth Sense?" But,
even here, the writer lapsed into mysticism half-way down the
column, bringing in instances of crystal-gazing and telepathy.
Even the dowsing-rod, which had seemed a good starting-point
for demonstrating the purely material nature of Michael's faculty, was also, it appeared, often claimed by the psychic school
and so did not clear the issue. Here inevitably cropped up the
old Aymar case, where the dowser is said to have followed the
trail of three murderers like a bloodhound from Lyons until
the French frontier stopped him. The writer had imagination,
however, if no logic. He concluded with a fantastically heightened pen-portrait of Michael's appearance and a quotation one
degree less trite than the coroner's:

"Weave a circle round him thrice
And close your eyes in holy dread,
For he on honey-dew hath fed
And drunk the milk of Paradise."

The little lines between Hilda's brows deepened in those few days. It was on her that there fell the weight of Michael's new phase, as upon her had fallen the weight of his bad days. The boy himself was half intoxicated by the sudden change, and more irresponsible than ever. He talked freely to reporters, and, though he was exasperated by their garbled accounts of what he had said, and had the humour to laugh heartily at the "honey-dew" account of himself, he did not learn reticence. Some of the reporters offered him money to give demonstrations, or to be photographed, and Hilda told me that he had accepted it before she knew of it and was spending it all on magnets and batteries. It seemed that he had been impatient to study magnetic effects for himself ever since the afternoon they had spent in Selver's laboratory.

For myself, I can say that I liked Bristowe better at this time than ever before. He was boyishly excited, but he had something of the disarming quality of an eager boy. His dark moroseness and bitterness seemed to vanish as if by magic. It was, of course, the other side of the same character, this exaggerated exultation at a little encouragement, the forward swing of the pendulum of the neurotic temperament. Nevertheless, a little natural charm began to glimmer in Michael Bristowe in those days, so that I began to wonder whether Hilda might not after all have been right in attributing his unfortunate traits to his peculiar circumstances, rather than to an innate tendency. With me he almost dropped the half sneer which was his usual manner.

Even that incalculable quality that was always present in him seemed less disconcerting.

About the exact nature of the encouragement he was receiving Michael was undiscriminating. It seemed to be enough for him at the moment that at last it was recognised that he was different from other people and could do things that they could not. It irritated him at times that the nature of the difference should be so absurdly misunderstood, but he did not see it as a disaster. It made Hilda, on the other hand, with her instinct for truth, extremely uneasy. She began to realise the true value of this teacup storm in the Press, though she did not feel entitled to discourage it.

"It will be over in a week's time," she said to me. "They are interested because Michael is associated with a popular crime, that's all. And, as there is to be no trial" (the suspected murderer had committed suicide as soon as the police suspicions began to turn from Michael to him) "there is nothing to keep up interest in it. And the only result is that, in spite of all we could say, everyone regards Michael as just an ordinary 'medium.' He's gone to a spiritualistic séance this evening. Mrs. Montalban-Smith got hold of him and made him promise yesterday. He went off laughing. But I don't like it."

Although I was glad enough to have Hilda to myself—another advantage I was deriving from Michael's sudden popularity—this news disturbed me.

"Couldn't you prevent it?" I said. "An impressionable youngster like Michael is the last person in the world who ought to go in for that sort of thing!"

"But I'm not afraid from that point of view," Hilda laughed. "You always mistake the nature of Michael's impressionability,

Ralph. Of course, he's temperamental and excitable and over-sensitive. But that is a very different matter from being easily taken in. Haven't you noticed that in matters of fact Michael has an uncanny instinct for what is genuine? I think it is his extra sense; he has an additional anchor cast into reality, as you might put it. He is a four-legged stool where most of us are three-legged, and we are far more likely to lose our balance than he is. If there's any faking, Michael won't be deceived by it."

"What's wrong, then?"

Her face became shadowed again. "It's all wrong that he should be associated with this kind of thing at all. It means that no one is beginning to understand what he really is. Everyone thinks he is just another medium like all the rest. The people it might have been worth while to convince will believe either that it's all been a fluke, or else that it's one of the spiritualistic phenomena that are best left to experts. And when all the excitement is over, I'm afraid for Michael—I'm afraid."

I could not say that I thought she had not reason to be so.

I went away and began to write an article setting out a philosophical view of Michael Bristowe's peculiarity, so far as I had been able to form one.

And thus I found myself involved in the necessity that I had shirked so long—the necessity to crystallise what I myself thought of Michael. The task was still repugnant to me, and I do not think anything but Hilda's anxiety would have brought me to it.

I found now how completely my ideas had changed during this period of half-wilful blindness. However I might cling to doubts of the value and importance of Michael's faculty, about its existence and activity I no longer had any sort of doubt.

Certainly, every one of the odd things that I had seen might, by a little straining, have been explained away by a determined sceptic (what can a determined sceptic not explain away?) as trickery, as guess-work, as coincidence. I knew in my heart that such interpretation would be wrong. I knew that Bristowe had a new faculty, or, more probably, a vast intensification of one which already existed incipiently in the human race. He was that thing we had forgotten to expect—a new mutation of the species. Such mutations had occurred throughout the ages in the development of life, vegetable and animal. Some had survived, accumulated and brought the race to other modes of existence. Countless numbers had failed to survive, crippled rather than helped by their peculiarity, or perhaps, crushed out by blind accident in spite of it. Even among men, even in historic times, there had been such—giants, strong men, men with tails and horns, beings whose sexual adjustments had differed, not always disadvantageously, from the normal ones. There had been the Nussbaumer brothers, who saw sounds in colour, not by a poetic fiction, but in sober fact; there had been Christian Heinecken, the child with the superhuman brain; calculating boys and prodigies of memory; there had been the subjects of Von Reichenbach's experiments. None of them, recent enough for us to know of, had "made good" in the racial sense. How would it be with Bristowe?

I did not say all this directly and definitely in the article I wrote. I wrote it cautiously, aiming at little beyond the clearing of the ground of the fantastic journalistic undergrowth which had overrun it. I made it the sort of article that critics call "subtle" and "suggestive." I told myself (as I afterwards explained to Hilda also) that it was necessary to begin in this manner, very quietly, in order to prepare people's minds, because they would not immediately accept the full implications of the thing. Ghosts, miracles, supernatural voices were well enough, because, of these things, however marvellous, they had heard before. But as regards a really new idea, I knew only too well the utter inhospitality of my fellow-countrymen.

But here a mental discomfort warns me that I must use my probe again. I realise that I was glad to have this excuse for not expressing my convictions too frankly. I did not know what was going to be the outcome of this business, and I did not want to commit myself too far. I knew that it would be useless to offer my article to the daily Press—my reputation is not one that carries any weight in those quarters. I intended to send it to the editor of the *Mentor*, a personal friend, with a note asking that it might, if possible, be put in the next issue while the subject was still topical. The *Mentor*, like most good weeklies, has a very small circulation. Nevertheless, it might do something among the more intelligent public to disperse the fog of supernaturalism in which Michael's achievement had been smothered. But if I made the article too positive, it might strain George Robert's friendship to put it in; and, even if he printed it, I might have reason to regret it. I signed it with initials only.

VII

THE MORNING AFTER I HAD DESPATCHED MY INSIGNIFI-
cant attempt to set Michael Bristowe right with the world,
I was sorry that I had put myself to so much trouble; for
it appeared that something far more consequential was in
process of happening to him. I saw it in the columns of *The
Daily Stunt* which, moved by a suggestive placard, I broke the
habit of a lifetime to buy. It asserted (and I have no doubt
with truth) that for days past the *Stunt* had been urging the
police authorities to make use of the young man who had
recently brought to light a notorious crime, in the investiga-
tions that were proceeding into the disappearance of Annie
Dukes, the girl who had mysteriously vanished some days
before from her home in a Cotswold village. It (the *Stunt*)
fully recognised that Michael Bristowe's methods were not
precisely orthodox—not those hallowed by the ancient (not to
say hidebound) traditions of Scotland Yard, but it (the *Stunt*)
for its part, judged by results, remembering that "there were
more things, etc…"

In fine, the *Stunt* had decided that, in default of official
action, it would itself, in the public interest, send the young
"clairvoyant" to the Cotswold village in question, paying all
expenses, and providing the escort of one of its most brilliant
correspondents, so that its readers might be informed of all
developments as they occurred from day to day.

In the evening, Hilda confirmed the news. Michael had consented to the expedition in a mood of mischievous compliance, persuaded by Cummings, the *Stunt* man who was to go with him. Whether the case would actually be one in which his faculty could give any assistance was, of course, very doubtful. Hilda, however, thought that even failure might be useful. She wanted at all costs to clear away the false impression that had become established about him.

I refrained from expressing my disagreement. It is a pathetic fallacy of youth that "one might as well have a shot at things. If it doesn't come off, there'll be no harm done." Harm is done by any failure, in loss of confidence and loss of prestige. If Michael failed in this, there would certainly be a loss of the latter. In his peculiar position it was most inexpedient that he should attempt anything he could not be sure of carrying through successfully. But, as it was too late to protest, I said nothing.

About those days that Michael spent in the Cotswolds I have, of course, no first-hand information, nor any account from Hilda. At her prompting I later approached Cummings for his version, and he passed on to me a little impatiently copies of the *Stunt* reports, and also the old notebook that he had used on this occasion, in which he had jotted down scraps of information and comment for his own benefit and, no doubt, possible future use. It is a curious document in many ways, and one which I think nobody but the typical journalist, to whom the things of yesterday are as dead as last year's lilies, would have cared to pass on to a comparative stranger. Some of the entries are in shorthand, and of no use to me, but many are in ordinary script. I take it that, like other journalists I have known, Cummings lapses into longhand when he is expressing any really vivid idea or impression.

This was in these later days—hardly more than a month ago. I began the reading with an almost painful eagerness. I felt that it might help to clear my own view if I could discover how Michael Bristowe appeared to this other man, this brilliant correspondent of the *Stunt*, who had passed a week in close companionship with him, and whose clearsightedness would not be obscured by the personal problem which affected my own. I finished my reading more mystified, if possible, by Cummings's personality than by Bristowe's.

It was natural, of course, that Michael should puzzle him from the first, but, in the best professional manner, he made a good thing of his bewilderment.

"One gets the impression," says his first despatch, "of a nice normal youth, even, perhaps, a little young for his age... This clairvoyant, this young seer, of whose achievements all the papers have been full for a week past, chose a comic weekly at the station bookstall, just as you or I might, chattered gaily to me in the first-class smoking compartment which the *Stunt* had placed at our disposal (he told me that it was the first time in his life that he had travelled first-class!), and attacked the excellent luncheon provided in the restaurant car with the appetite of a newly released schoolboy. And then, as I was about to help myself to the apple with which (as Dr. Merriman, the *Daily Stunt* health expert, assures us) every meal ought to conclude, young Bristowe said quietly, 'Don't take that one; it's rotten inside.'

"The apple looked fresh and rosy; if there was any outward and visible sign of its inner corruption, I could not find it. I held on to it, of course, out of curiosity, but took the precaution of slicing it in half immediately. And there, sure enough, I found that I had interrupted a most lively luncheon party in full swing.

"Michael Bristowe was watching me with a quiet smile when I looked up.

"'How did you know?' I demanded.

"'I just knew,' with a slight lift of his shoulders.

"And that was the only explanation I could get of this odd little incident.

"'Well, but,' I reasoned with myself, 'this youth comes from the country; perhaps he knows more about apples than I do.'

"Are even one's thoughts safe from Michael Bristowe? Anyhow, a moment later, he was insisting on describing to me the exact contents of my pocket—a chaos of which I had imagined that I alone possessed the key. And though he protested that he could form no idea as to what was in the letters that were among them, I did not feel completely reassured. If he was able to divine what I had in my pockets—notecase, knife, cough lozenges, keys, and so on—it seems only reasonable to suppose that he would be able to make a pretty good guess at the contents of the letters also. I feared his disclaimer was mere politeness, and felt glad that at the moment my conscience was comparatively unencumbered!

"I rejoiced still more that my withers were unwrung when this truly terrible young man informed me later that the elderly gentleman of military appearance who shared our compartment for a short distance was wearing corsets with steel in them, and that the pearls of the opulent-looking lady who had been sitting near us at luncheon were imitation. What a disturbing element Michael Bristowe would be to introduce into smart society! These two last assertions I was naturally unable to verify; but I have personally no doubt as to their accuracy.

"But a truce to such frivolities! These trifles seem hardly worthy of the spiritual genius of one who may turn out to be the greatest clairvoyant of all time. (For some reason Bristowe objects to the word, and will have it that his gift is 'purely physical'—but we shall not quarrel about words if the goods are delivered.) This evening we reached Sandford, and to-morrow we begin on the task of tracing the missing girl. I cannot believe that, with Michael Bristowe's co-operation, it can prove a very long and arduous task."

Elsewhere he describes Michael's appearance—a description a little at odds with the "nice normal youth" effect—but then, this is in a passage set in a more mysterious key. Cummings's descriptive passages are not always without talent. He brings out well enough the lithe dangerous vitality of Michael's light figure, his quick movements, the lowering effect of his heavy brows, and the sudden flashes of almost demonish mischief that lit up his face when he smiled.

Two days later his first impression of Michael seems to have been considerably modified. This appears even in the article published in the *Stunt*.

"Let no one imagine that it is altogether a light matter to be associated with Michael Bristowe in an expedition of this sort. The young clairvoyant is not a holiday companion. There is another side to his marvellous powers. He radiates vitality, he quivers with sensitiveness. Where one man, startled, would jump a foot, Bristowe jumps three. He is like a man without a skin. One feels, indeed, that he is acted upon by influences outside our limited ken… Well, all this, of course, is to be expected. Genius, of whatever kind, is never easy to live with. And of Bristowe's genius I have less doubt than ever. I can truly say that he is quite unlike anyone else that I have ever happened to meet. It is true that we have been here two days and so far without definite result, yet no one who has been privileged as I have…" and so on.

The remarks in the notebook on this same date are more succinct. "Can't stand much more of this. If it isn't over in a day or two, must ask S. to relieve me. B. seems made of quicksilver and getting on my nerves. Shall want a holiday when we have finished."

At the same time I utterly fail to make out exactly what Cummings himself thought of Michael Bristowe—that is, what he, the man, really made of the strange disturbing being superficially so like ourselves, yet with his mysterious difference. All his comments, even those intended for his private purposes, have a professional bias; they deal with the business in hand; there is no attempt to see the thing in its universal bearings, to find a personal point of view. I am almost driven to wonder whether, after all, there was such a thing as Cummings the man—whether it is, after all, possible to be one of the *Stunt*'s most brilliant correspondents, and to remain at the same time a living soul with an individual point of view. Certainly this remark about the quicksilver, with its faint suggestion of the panic which I believe no one who came into contact with Michael Bristowe can have entirely escaped, is the nearest thing to an expression of personal opinion which I can find in the material I have to hand.

In his second report to the *Daily Stunt* Cummings described their interview with the bereaved mother. It was first-rate "sob stuff," and he let himself go over it—the broken-hearted, grey-haired mother in her poor little cottage, imploring the young seer (Cummings obviously relished that word) to find her lost child for her, indulging in pathetic reminiscences, giving way to her grief, calling in sympathetic neighbours to support her story. Michael's part in all this, however, as described, I find a little unconvincing. It does not sound like the Michael Bristowe I knew. More illuminating again on this point is the parallel comment of the notebook:

"Had curious scene with B. after visit to Mrs. D. Seems upset about it. Insists I have misrepresented him, and that he'll only find girl if she is dead. Hope she *is* dead, in that case. Can't afford to have this a wild goose chase. Young fool made himself quite ill. Fiendish temper." Poor Cummings! He had my sympathy as I read this unwonted expansion into sentiment. At such moments, no one but Hilda could ever do anything with Michael.

Michael's methods also nonplussed the *Stunt* correspondent. He had expected the usual paraphernalia of spiritualism—a séance, crystal-gazing, planchette—that kind of thing. These would have provided him with material for picturesque description. When they were rejected, he offered to get Michael some of the girl's clothing, having a notion that mediums often "got the scent," as he put it, in that way; and was annoyed when Michael laughed. Michael's genuine search of the neighbourhood for the body of the girl, in case it was anywhere concealed, exasperated a mind to whom abnormal faculties meant dramatically quick results, if they meant anything at all.

"Paraded country-side again from morning to night," the notebook complains pathetically. "B. makes the most extraordinary remarks. Passed over a limestone hill yesterday, and he grinned and said how 'quaint' it was. Beginning to wonder if he isn't just an uncommon sort of lunatic, after all. Found my lost penknife to-day. Went straight to it under the edge of the carpet. (Work this up for *Stunt*.) Seems to have obsession that this case must be exactly like last, and that girl must be buried somewhere in neighbourhood... Haven't done so much walking in years. (N.B.—Better begin to prepare *Stunt* for possible failure.)"

It was certainly hard on the brilliant correspondent. He had got his man there, a first-class situation, occasions for impressiveness, wonder, pathos, humour at every turn, and the wretched youth refused to co-operate. He just went on with his systematic parading of the country-side, without even the panoply of a divining-rod, and nothing happened. Cummings became pathetic. It wasn't as though Bristowe couldn't, if he would. There was the penknife episode. There were odd little things all the time. For instance, apart from finding things, Bristowe knew when anyone was coming long before even the dogs knew. (This gave occasion for a vivid little vignette for the *Stunt*.) These had been all very well for the first day or two. But they were wearing thin. Cummings had to make bricks without straw in his daily despatches. And he was sick to death of the comforts of "The Red Lion."

And then, one day, apparently came illumination—a chaffing letter (fastened bodily into the notebook) from a colleague, asking how long he meant to stay rusticating with his pet medium, and when the said medium was going to get busy. It also remarked that he (the colleague) had been talking to a friend who was interested in spirits (a little joke here, of course), and *he* (the friend) said that Bristowe had been examined by a prominent spiritualistic circle just before he left Town, and that they hadn't thought much of him. He had only "a very limited clairvoyance," they said, and hadn't the sense to recognise those who had more psychic power than himself. He had behaved very boorishly, asked all sorts of impertinent questions, and finally rushed out in the middle of a most important "communication." His discovery of the Morland murder must have been mere lucky chance.

To Cummings, the inference seems to have been obvious. That is the strange part of it. The letter did not destroy his faith in Michael's capacity to discover something if he wished—those odd little things that had cropped up had made too strong an impression for that. Cummings's mind worked on another and, to me, a fantastically tortuous line. As he saw it—Michael was in bad odour in his own profession; his poverty and difficulties were obvious to anyone who had visited him at his London lodgings, as had Cummings; and now he had had a slice of luck that had brought him notoriety and a chance to make hay while the sun shone; apart from this affair, his prospects were evidently poor. Obviously then, it was a great advantage to him to be enjoying the *Stunt's* hospitality even at a "Red Lion" standard of living; obviously, he would be in no hurry to bring to a close this period of peace and plenty.

I suppose that an eye for character is not a necessity to a publicity machine. Yet, apart from the peculiar circumstances, I find it difficult to understand how any man of average intelligence could have suspected Michael Bristowe of this sort of trickery. There are men whose faces are a warning not to trust them, there are men whose faces are neutral—ordinary decent men who will lie and shuffle under varying degrees of pressure, and there are the very few whom one knows at once are incapable of artifice, whose very faults lie in the opposite direction—in pride and recklessness, and contempt for what their fellows can do. Michael Bristowe had some qualities detestable enough, but chicanery was not one of them.

And, then, too, Cummings had obviously acquired no more idea than when he started as to the real nature of Michael's powers. He still thought of him as what he called a "spiritual genius," capable of revealing the whereabouts of Annie Dukes by supernormal methods, if he would. Evidently, Cummings's experience on the *Stunt* had not suggested to him that even "spiritual genius" can afford indifference to considerations of £ *s. d.*

But what is the use of trying to follow the mental twists of the *Stunt*'s star correspondent? Especially as I have no direct evidence. I merely infer that he must have thought something after this fashion from the next amazing entry in the notebook, after the record of the fatal letter:

"Gave B. to understand that he would lose nothing by finding A. D. promptly."

There is added a sentence that did not surprise me. "Glared at me like nothing on earth, and left the room without a word. Don't mind, if only it has penetrated." The last sentence made me smile. One had to assure oneself that one did not mind when Bristowe glared at one. I knew that already, and it bolstered up my self-respect to feel that even a pachyderm like the *Stunt* correspondent, even in his laconic private notes, had been impelled to make a similar concession.

The next entry is worded in full, and shows agitation even in the writing. "Well, he's gone off, and though it's a failure for me, I'm glad. I couldn't have stood another day of it. I don't know if the *Stunt* will publish my last report."

There is no more to do with Bristowe in the notebook. The *Stunt* apparently did not publish the last despatch, to which Cummings refers. The next morning it was deeply interested in a war threat in the Far East, and in proposals for ending the latest strike. But Providence had looked after its chief under-study. Before he left the village that evening, I think Cummings must have had an interview with the local constable, and heard the news which was published in all the papers the next morning. Annie Dukes had been found, together with the young man with whom she had eloped, staying in a seaport town some fifty miles away from her home. It seemed that Mrs. Dukes' knowledge of her daughter's activities had not been exhaustive. The police, following up a clue suggested by an old school-friend of Annie's, had worked on it patiently until they ran the young couple to earth. The *Stunt* was accordingly able to publish a short obscure paragraph saying that, the girl having been found, the services of Mr. Bristowe, the clairvoyant detective, who had been engaged on the case on behalf of the *Stunt*, had become unnecessary, and Mr. Bristowe had already left the village.

VIII

So, ONCE AGAIN, AS IN THE INTERVIEW WITH OLD Rosenheimer and as from his job at Harding's, Michael Bristowe flung royally away, back to poverty and obscurity—and to dependence, material and moral, upon Hilda. For that was what it amounted to. Michael's boom was over. Press excitement over the murder case had died down during the last week. There was a little gibing and laughter over the conclusion of the new one in other papers than the *Stunt*. My article had appeared obscurely in the *Mentor* without perceptible result. Michael's post-bag, which Hilda had dealt with during his absence, had shrunk to manageable size. Lamenting mothers no longer besought him to come and cure their ailing children, people who suspected their neighbours of secret atrocities directed their stream of anonymity (no doubt) elsewhere; he ceased to interest supremely the inmates of asylums and homes for the feeble-minded.

I knew little then of what had actually happened in the Cotswold village. Michael had sent only brief postcards to Hilda. The *Stunt* reports had been amusing, but their high colouring was visible to the naked eye. When I saw that the affair had ended in a somewhat comic fiasco, and that Michael had come home, if not a definite failure, at any rate nothing of a success, I stayed away in sheer cowardice, leaving Hilda alone to deal with him.

The chorus of gibes went on for a day or two. It was too good an opportunity for sly hits at the *Stunt* to be lost. And Michael had, of course, done himself no good with the other papers when he had accepted the commission in the first place. The thing culminated, two days after his return to London, in a column article in one of the more weighty and expensive Conservative journals, headed "Unconscious Observation," by a "Special Correspondent."

The article began by suggesting that all water-diviners obtain their results by acute observation of geological formations. This has always been the favourite sceptical theory of dowsing, though there are facts that are difficult to square with it—such facts, for instance, as that some dowsers can work blindfold, that there have been child-dowsers, and that springs have been discovered under buildings. However, the writer was able to quote instances and authority in favour of his theory; those that did not favour it, he refrained from mentioning. There are people, he continued, who have abnormally acute sight; they notice tiny indications that escape others, and, consciously or unconsciously, they make inferences from what they see. Might not some such hypothesis account for Michael Bristowe's discovery in the original instance (as also for his failure in the second) more reasonably than wild theories of supernatural powers? Minute signs, undetectable by ordinary observers, would suggest to him that something had taken place at the fatal spot, that the ground had been disturbed, perhaps (as, indeed, one of the detectives subsequently discovered), that the bushes had been pushed aside, that something untoward had occurred. People of this type were rarely of very stable mentality, and such indications, if he noticed them ("no doubt,

unconsciously"), might well account for the agitation of the
young "medium." The parenthetic phrase, "no doubt, unconsciously," here inevitably suggested the opposite possibility to
the reader—that Bristowe might have deliberately exploited
public credulity—an effect emphasised farther on in the article by a gentle suggestion (the occasion for which was left to
the imagination) that it was undesirable, in the present state
of opinion, that claimants of "psychic" powers should accept
money for their demonstrations—if they wished their claims
to be taken seriously.

I must confess that it was beautifully done. Quietly, deli-
cately, with learning and humour, it explained away Michael's
feat until nothing was left of it. Subtly it led up, without com-
mitting itself, to the reflection that, in a venal world, venality
was, on the whole, a more probable explanation than a hitherto
unheard-of faculty. Nine hundred and ninety-nine men out of
a thousand would have said that this was an entirely balanced
impartial exposition of the case. It is not especially to my credit
that I happen to be the thousandth. Though I have never myself
experienced the sordid pressure which drives men to do this
sort of thing, it is a part of my professional equipment to know
how it is done. Almost imperceptible exaggerations and suppres-
sions, touches of irony, given, perhaps, by the mere transposi-
tion of two words or the insertion of inverted commas—it is
an infinitely more subtle affair than the most skilful speech of
the most brilliant barrister—and the thing—the new art, the
eccentric preacher, the unpopular movement—has become a
sham and a laughing-stock. Exquisitely transfixed, the victims
writhe helplessly. Unless they have a thorough training in logical
analysis, nowhere can they point and say, "This is unfair," "This

is misleading." If they have such a training and do so point, no one will pay any attention to them.

It is highly skilled labour, this, a cut above the Cummings level—a form of prostitution, of course, but a very refined and delicate prostitution, an occasion for the *lorettes*, not the *grisettes*, of the profession. Sometimes it is even done not solely for money, but for malice, or for notoriety—or for love of the work.

Half-way down the column a civil sneer suggested that even the intelligentsia were not always so ungullible as one might expect. Of course, they did not believe in ghosts, or anything of that sort, only in vague possibilities, unfathomed depths, potentialities of abnormal capacities in human nature. Well, vaguenesses and potentialities were, no doubt, very useful sometimes, but need we really fall back upon them in the present instance?

The allusion to my own article in the *Mentor* was unmistakable; in fact, my journalistic experience suggested to me that a more definite reference had been cut editorially just at this point, probably in order to prevent a paper run by opposed interests from receiving a free advertisement.

I had no difficulty in identifying the "Special Correspondent." The article had a certain mannerism in it—a peculiar use of the rhetorical question always beginning, "And so we are to…?" Henry Selver was some ten years my senior, and, for a short period of my callow youth, I had admired and imitated his style.

I did not need confirmation, but I went to Hilda that evening and asked her whether she had seen Selver recently. I found that she had met him at the beginning of the week, and that he had been cool and off-hand, obviously offended that she had, after all, allowed Michael's "boom" to start without him. I decided to show her the article (which she had not seen), and to tell her my conviction about its authorship.

Looking back now, I date almost from this moment the stiffening, the touch of sternness, that began to pass into Hilda's youthfulness. Her partisanship of Michael Bristowe, eager as it had been, had remained a flexible thing; to one less intimately concerned than I was, I imagine that it might even have seemed rather charming. From now on, it began to develop a flavour of fanaticism. I had not foreseen this effect of Selver's treachery. After all, it was not the fall of an idol from a pedestal—she had never, I knew, imagined him to be a champion *sans peur et sans reproche*. Nevertheless, as I realised later, to young people like Hilda, there are depths to which it is almost inconceivable that any human being whom they have seen or spoken to can descend. Such a fall is like crime, loathsome disease, divorce. One reads about such things—they do not happen in one's own neighbourhood. This was a disillusionment about human nature in general, rather than about Henry Selver in particular—a moral shock. It was one of those experiences which put forward one's age years at a bound, if one acquiesces in them. The indomitably young will, of course, fight instead, and fight fanatically.

I don't know whether I ought to reproach myself for having made the revelation to her at all. I do not think so. It is true that I did not realise the probable effect. But I was governed by practical considerations. It was almost certain that something or someone would call her attention to the article sooner or later; or Michael might see it, and its effect upon him (which

might well be disastrous) might take her unawares. I do not
think I could have done otherwise. It was merely another trick
of jesting Providence that I should have been the agent to
inflict this damage upon her. Yet, if I had realised then exactly
what I was doing, I might have been able to mitigate it, to
say the word which would have been the antidote—for there
usually is such a word, but it is only the spiritual genius (to
use Cummings's favourite expression) who can find and use it
at the precise moment of need. It is the curse of the analytic
temperament, such as mine, to understand these things only
when it is too late. I had already reached the essential truth
about this episode in the intervening months, before Hilda, at
the time when she came to talk more freely to me, showed it
to me herself. It would have been better for my peace of mind
never to have realised it at all.

At the time, I felt merely a vague discomfort and anxiety at
the silence, lasting several seconds, in which she received my
news. Then, without making any comment on Selver's part
in the affair, she began to discuss what was to be done. I was
ready enough to help. Although Selver's action was not a shock
to me in the sense that it was so to her, I was angry enough,
and my hitherto grudging adherence to Michael's cause was
stiffened. Unfortunately, there is little that one can do in such
circumstances. The article, infinitely more damaging than a
column of direct abuse, was a hundred miles on the safe side
of the libel law. We might, and did, try counterblasts in the
other papers, and a protest in that one. I don't know whether
Hilda expected much from this. I did not, and I was justified.
The Press was tired of us. Our efforts appeared not at all, or
abridged, in obscure corners.

We agreed, as we sat there talking, that Michael should not know of the article, if it could be avoided. Hilda was anxious that the insinuations against his integrity should be kept from him. She did not tell me all that Michael had told her about his expedition with Cummings, but I gathered that there had been trouble of a similar nature there, and that its effect on Michael had been dismaying. It was unfortunate that he should have accepted money from reporters in the first place, but, as the reporters were now leaving him alone, there was no danger of his repeating the mistake. Whereas, if we let him know what use had been made of his indiscretion, we could not tell what he might do.

I saw that Hilda paled slightly as she considered the possible effect of the revelation on Michael. It was my first intimation that she too had her uncertainties and hesitations before the incalculable element in him. She had always seemed to have him so well in hand. Now she added quickly, with a perplexed smile, as if to cover her misgivings:

"Looking after Michael is rather like running an egg-and-spoon race."

I broke out and swore, "D—— him. He's worrying you to death!"

"He *is* worrying me," Hilda smiled again. "He'd have worried anyone these last few days…" She broke off, evidently deciding to tell me no more of that. "Don't you see how it is, Ralph? He's had a fortnight of recognition, almost of adulation, after a lifetime of cold-shouldering. I should doubt if he has even spoken to as many people in the whole of his life before as in these last few weeks. He has been almost a pariah from childhood, owing to his queerness. And that in itself has made him still more sensitive to social atmosphere. Then, for this bit of time, he has been lionised. And now he is back again where he was—in a dingy lodging, with no money, nothing to do, no prospects, and completely neglected."

I stared at her, sickened and irritated that this youth's disturbing existence should be so constantly with us. I was drawn in by this time beyond remedy, but I had still my moments of revulsion. Lately, I had had several quiet evenings, like this one, alone with Hilda, but Michael's absence had never relieved us of his company. She did not say any more, but I knew what the tightening of her lips meant. She was alone again in her conviction of Michael's importance to humanity. Well, then, single-handed, if necessary, she would fight the world on his behalf, including the morbid devils of his own nature; and, if she went under, she would go under fighting.

There seemed to be no end to it.

I laughed, though with no gaiety, when she glanced anxiously at the clock and exclaimed, "He can't be coming round to-night. I must go and see what's the matter."

It was a wild autumn night, raining and blowing, but I did not waste my energy in a protest. I merely told her that I meant to take a taxi home and would run her round on the way. She got up at once with a word of thanks, and went to put on her outdoor things. It was almost equivalent to turning me out, and the unconsciousness with which it was done made it the more stinging. Only her evident anxiety kept me from sarcastic speech. I made up my mind that, at least, I would not leave her to make an indefinite stay at Bristowe's rooms.

"I'm going to wait and run you back again when you've seen him," I told her doggedly as she got down before the dingy lodging-house.

There followed the inevitable small altercation, but I held to my point; and Hilda, glancing uneasily at the darkened house, cut it short with a last adjuration, and rang the bell. As she vanished inside, she called "goodnight" to me.

It must have been nearly an hour that I waited in the chilly damp, pacifying with difficulty the restive taxi-driver. I might have known better, I thought bitterly, than to suppose that the fact of my waiting in the rain would make Hilda cut short an interview with Michael Bristowe. Unreasonably, since she had told me not to stay, I worked myself into a fever of impatience, as I tramped the pavement or cowered out of the storm in a corner of the cab, while I piled up mentally the cutting things that I would say when she appeared at last.

I was contemplating an attack upon the door myself, or whether I should not make the driver use his horn, when at last she slipped out quietly and came across the pavement towards me. The light of a street lamp shone across her face for a moment, and all the fierce sentences in my mind withered and died, leaving only pity and apprehension. It was not just that she was pale and her features sharp with exhaustion. It was the curse of Michael again. It hung about her in an indefinable manner, as if she were involved in some fourth dimensional tragedy, intangible, but not utterly imperceptible, to ordinary humanity.

But I suppressed my sense of fantasy in the face of Hilda's obvious need. She let me help her into the car, hardly seeming to recognise that I had waited against her expressed wish, and sank back into the corner.

We drove back to the flat almost in silence. She merely said to me after a moment:

"He'd seen it."

I knew that already. "Is it all right?" I asked.

"All right now." That was all she had to tell me.

A moment later I saw with thankfulness her own door closing behind her.

I X

THAT EVENING, WHEN I TOOK HILDA ROUND TO MICHAEL
Bristowe's rooms, waited for her, and drove her home
again, was, I think, except for one other, the strangest that I
spent in the whole of that strange time. I had not seen Michael
at all, but I felt as if I had. I had seen his presence reflected
in Hilda, and it was strong enough to make my mind reel
in the intellectual vertigo with which Michael's personality
had more than once affected me. I had actually that sense
of struggling on the dark edge of reality which anæsthetics
will sometimes produce. It is odd that Michael's glamour (I
do not know how else to call it) should have been so strong
at this particular moment—a moment of defeat and humiliation, of disproportionate reaction to a sordid newspaper
insult. True, it was an evening to encourage an overstrained
imagination; moreover, I was unduly sensitive at the time to
any effect produced upon Hilda; and I have never seen her
so white, so nearly at the end of her resources, as when she
came to me across the pavement and let me almost lift her
into the waiting taxi. But, when all is said, there remains that
element of skewness which entered into everything in which
Michael Bristowe was concerned. Nothing that happened to
him could be quite like the same thing happening to another
man... I spent a feverish night, full of vague, demoralising
dream horrors.

And then, in less than twenty-four hours, the whole situation was transmuted. In the person of one little man, a sun of commonplaceness rose upon the darkness of our problem. Things became safe and stable; Michael was a clever youth with actual money in his pockets and more at the bank, and prospects in the future. The blatant, cheerful light of money shone upon us; mystery vanished before it.

Our sun rose from the West in the shape of Horace G. Plumer, a small spare American with a lined face, bright eyes, jerky movements and a penetrable mind. He came to me with an introduction from my sister Mildred, who, having married a minor peer, has a wide acquaintance among Americans. Plumer was interested in oil; he had come over to form a syndicate for the working of a hitherto untouched area in Eastern Europe. He had read my article in the *Mentor* the week before, and had somehow discovered my authorship.

Rather annoyed, I enquired politely what my literary activities could have to do with the oil in which he was interested.

"Well, Mr. Standring, if they haven't anything, I've come on a wild goose chase, and troubled you for nothing," and the little American shut his mouth with a good-humoured snap.

To account for the effect of this speech of Plumer's upon me, I have to remember the previous weeks and our terrifying sense of helplessness. I had had it throughout the whole business, the same choking helplessness as had oppressed me in the dreams of the last night. But especially during this last phase of Michael's sudden notoriety, its climax and slump, it had gripped Hilda, as I knew, as well as myself. How Michael himself felt about anything one could never be sure; in some way, complex, gifted, incomprehensible as he was, I always conceived of him as living a more immediate life than we, more directly concerned with the things of the moment, with less compulsion to estimate values or calculate results. But, for us, these weeks had been a fight with shadows, a nightmare obstacle race. How can one express it? Anyone conscious of an important truth, the convinced apostle of a new religion; the explorer with true, though incredible, tales; the genius unable to make the world see the new form of beauty so resplendent to himself, might feel something the same. Yet it was not so much that the world refused to believe us as that it would not stop to understand us. It was like the conversations that one may hear in any Customs house and frontier station in the tourist season, in which each side shouts louder and louder, answering questions which the other has not asked, commenting on statements which the other has not made. It was the irrelevancy that terrified. The people who thronged around Michael and excited themselves about him were actually interested neither in him, nor in the nature of any exceptional power that he might have; they were interested in being in at the latest sensation, or in getting material for a good story, or in collecting the latest celebrity; in making use of him in some way for their special purposes. It was a matter of no significance to them whether a sixth sense existed, or was possible to humanity, or not. Like all losing combats with the intangible, this one brought one almost to a state of panic at last.

And now I found that Horace G. Plumer actually understood; that he really listened to what was said to him and took it in; that he had read my article and understood it, understood not only its statements, but its implications, all that I had intended remotely to suggest by it; that he had then proceeded to read what other papers said about Michael ("I know how much salt to put to a newspaper report by this time—we get good practice in that at home," he told me), and, following the history of the abortive *Stunt* expedition, had seen that all this had borne out my thesis. As I listened, I made a comprehensive mental apology to Plumer's nation. My ideas about Americans underwent a revolution in five minutes. And though I continued to see him throughout our association (as we British are, I think, too apt to see foreigners) objectively, as an odd, jerky, little figure in two dimensions thrown gesticulating on a screen for my diversion, I was ashamed of my myopia.

I have often thought that, while we Northern Europeans are like unformed adolescents as compared with the Latin races with their finish and *savoir faire*, their air of inborn experience, we have, on the other hand, like adolescents, the possibilities of growth still open to us. We are still capable of new impressions and of wider experience. Those others may be said to be "finished" in more senses than one. Now, it occurred to me that, as we are to the Latins, so, perhaps, are the Americans to us. They are still capable of seeing freshly without preconception, in situations where we are not. I saw now that there might be another side to the crudely yelling American journals of my detestation, and to those countless American books which present hundreds of pages of semi-scientific platitudes as if they were fresh flowers of the intellect with the morning dew upon them. I even forgave Plumer when he made an excursion into orthodox Yankee facetiousness (which, to do him justice, happened seldom), and told me that he agreed with the Bard "that there were more things running about loose in the world than Dr. Freud ever prised up out of an Unconscious." And, if he ever came up against one of those that had dollars in it, he added, he wasn't going to say "Run away, you've no call to exist," to any little phenomenon of that sort.

It was in following this principle, Plumer had come to the conclusion that Michael Bristowe might very well prove a useful asset to a man interested in oil. His syndicate, he told me, would not be ready to operate for another three or four months, but, if he found that Bristowe was likely to be an oil-finder, he would make it worth his while to wait for them.

He could hardly know, I thought, of the situation to which Michael was now reduced, and it was certainly not my business to tell him. On the other hand, I had no inclination to act as Michael's salesman. Any handling of Michael's affairs was like playing with a hedgehog, and I had had enough of it. Nevertheless, it would be tempting Providence to send any prospective employer to Michael's own rooms. I decided to take him round at once to Hilda, and pass on my responsibility as quickly as possible.

I ought, of course, to have warned Hilda of our coming, but it was already late afternoon, and I did not wish to let Plumer's offer remain unclinched an hour longer than was necessary. Thus it was that we came in upon Michael lying on the couch, his face the colour of lead, while Hilda was bending over him, giving him brandy. We were shown straight in by the little maidservant—there was, as I knew, nowhere else for her to put us, even if she had had sufficient discretion—this cramping lack of privacy involved in cheap living was one of the things that had most distressed me on Hilda's behalf, and from which I longed to take her away.

What Michael had been doing I never discovered; in fact, never asked. I preferred not to know. In that glimpse it seemed to me that there had been something not quite normal about the pupils of his eyes. Then Hilda, coming to meet us, asked us, with a pathetically youthful touch of dignity, to talk to her on the landing.

Plumer's good-nature was admirable. He had obviously the American instinct to put through business in the shortest possible space of time; yet, when I had explained the object of our visit to Hilda, he suggested that, as Mr. Bristowe appeared to be unwell, the interview had, perhaps, better be postponed until the next day. I am sure that if he had been looking at me he must have seen the jar at my heart as I heard the suggestion, reflected in my face. I had to suppress an impulse to seize him by the collar, at all costs to keep him there until he was committed beyond backing out. Hilda must surely have felt a corresponding jar, but certainly it did not show in her face. She even hesitated a moment. "I think he could see you now," she said finally, and asked us to excuse her a moment while she made sure.

Michael was still on the couch when we went back into the room, but the unnatural slackness of his attitude was gone. He was drawn together tensely, his eyes bright with the suspicious watchfulness of a wild animal that expects to be baited. I braced myself for trouble.

And then, as always with Michael, the unexpected occurred. From the moment that the little man stepped forward with his card and "Pleased to meet you, Mr. Bristowe," as Hilda introduced him, a spirit of uproarious mirth seemed to surge up in the strange being on the couch.

It rose in his eyes visibly like a tidal wave as he looked at the American, and was just held from breaking while he asked with quiet politeness:

"And what can I do for you, Mr. Plumer?"

Plumer was as always simple and definite. He told Michael what he had heard about him, and what he wanted of him, and added placidly, while Hilda and I drew in our breath sharply, that, of course, he had to make sure before striking any bargain that it was not all a fake, and that Mr. Bristowe really did know more than the next man.

"You want to know what I know?" Michael's voice shook with the rising storm of glee. "Well, I know…" and then it broke—a cyclone of mirthful rhapsody: "I know…" and he began to tell Horace Plumer some of the things he knew. I realised, as I listened, that I had been let off easily in the past. He told him what clothing he was wearing, what was in his pockets and in his dispatch-case, what he had had for lunch and how long ago, that he suffered from dyspepsia, and that one of his teeth needed stopping. Far worse and more intimate things than these he told him, becoming more and more outrageous, gusty laughter sweeping nearer and nearer to the surface.

And Horace Plumer stood his ground, smiling imperturbably, politely waiting for him to finish.

Abruptly, Michael changed his note. "What I know…" His voice was suddenly lost, dreamy, yet with a rushing undercurrent. I cannot say whether the drug which (as I suspected) he had been taking was influencing him. It is quite probable; but, on the other hand, the fantastic nature of his own personality might in itself do anything at any moment with Michael Bristowe.

"What I know... How can I tell you?... You can't see, or
feel it... You live in a universe with little hard limits... You
know nothing... This room is a prison to you... You can't feel
the sunset against the wall outside... or the people moving...
that cat going downstairs... or the water in the pipes... Even
when you are outside, there is nothingness... the ocean of
movement... Shifting formations... lines of energy... the great
waves... ripples crossing... patterns coming and going... It's all
nothing to you."

He was getting excited again. He spoke as I had never heard
him speak before. I cannot remember much of it, for, of course,
I could not follow it. Bristowe had no natural mastery of words.
They came now, disjointed, as if they were weapons wrested
from armed enemies in a life-and-death struggle. Some of
them he must have got from the scientific books that Selver
had lent him. Others seemed to have almost that simple violent
imagery which comes at the point where the emotional stress
of common people meets the supreme imaginative effort of
great poets.

"It is all solid and hard to you," he came back to that, looking round at us with a sort of mirthful pity. "Solid and hard...
throwing you back... you can't get through... Solid!... Are you
solid, do you think, Mr. Horace G. Plumer?" He suddenly fixed
the little American. "Do you think so now, really? After what
I've told you?... You're a ghost, I tell you... A ghost, if you only
knew it. A ghost with one back braces button of metal and the
other of horn!" And he laughed uproariously.

After that, for a moment he lay back silent, exhausted from
his laughter. No one spoke. Plumer was still standing, his
small bright eyes fixed with calm interest on Bristowe. Hilda

had been all this time behind the head of the couch looking down at Michael; the position of her hands as they rested on the upholstery sketched an instinctive attitude of support to the limp figure below.

"Well, Mr. Plumer,"—Michael sat up again after a moment, and addressed him in a perfectly matter-of-fact tone—"are you satisfied? Do you think that I know more than the next man?"

"No doubt about that, Mr. Bristowe," the hearty accents came with a startling effect of anticlimax. "I should say you know quite a lot. At the same time, the question for me is whether you'll be able to locate oil, say, three hundred feet underground, and tell us it's three hundred. Now, if you've no objection, to a few little tests—there's a useful patch of ground I can borrow not far out of this city—say, one day next week. We can't have the real conditions, of course, but I'll take that risk…"

I turned in a panic of apprehension to Michael. He stared at Plumer for a moment and then began to laugh quietly again as if with an uncontrollable secret amusement.

"Well…" Another abrupt change, this time to a sudden business-like sharpness: "What are you going to offer me if I do what you want?"

Plumer was prompt. "A thousand dollars down for the option of your services next spring. And then three thousand a year—that's six hundred pounds—if we take you on then."

"You'll give me two hundred pounds now, if I agree?" There was a shrill insistency in Michael's tone that was very unpleasant to hear. This sudden transition to obvious greed was the most disconcerting of all the moods that he had shown us in almost the same number of minutes. His eyes, fixed on Plumer, shone with the bright, covetous, almost lustful light that one sees too often in these days when a man's whole welfare frequently depends on how much he can sell.

I turned my back, and Hilda must have seen my disgust, for she murmured to me deprecatingly, "It's his magnets, Ralph."

For that moment I did not care what it was, or what Michael was—it was an ugly exhibition. Plumer, on the other hand, took it as unconcernedly as he had taken everything else. "As soon as you've satisfied me in the little tests I've mentioned, and signed a paper that I'll have ready, Mr. Bristowe, you shall have the cheque the same day," he assured Michael.

"That's settled then," said Michael Bristowe. He turned his face to the wall and shut his eyes.

The next time that I saw Bristowe he seemed to have dwindled. All impressiveness had gone from him. He was a professional oil-finder, with a niche in the structure of society and a market value. And he almost looked the part—young, fresh, with even a kind of spruceness. It was always like that with him. His face was always completely characterised by the expression of the moment. In a melancholic mood, he looked ill of a mortal disease; if something happened to provoke his mischievous grin, he immediately assumed the appearance of a healthy youngster years younger than his actual age. Hilda was obviously pleased at the improvement. I wondered if she was also conscious of the accompanying loss of personal effect, but I do not imagine that she was. There was never anything even remotely "psychic" about Hilda. Certainly Michael himself was not aware of it, or quite regardless, if he was. I saw him for only a few minutes on this occasion. He had run in to Hilda's flat and pressed upon her with loud-voiced cheerfulness a list of things that he wanted her to order for him in Town and a blank cheque to pay for them. And he was off again like a bird on the wing, with hardly a word to me. Hilda told me that now that he again had money to spend on it, he could hardly think of anything but his magnetic apparatus, and would scarcely have had sufficient meals if she had not kept a watch on him.

The next two or three months were the best part for me of those years in which the distresses of a lifetime seem to be concentrated. At last there seemed to be a favourable tide in my affairs. Plumer seemed to have come in like an odd little guardian angel. Michael Bristowe seemed to be at last placed and started. Contrary to my fears, Plumer had not been in the least disconcerted by his first most unprepossessing glimpse of Michael. I have never met anyone more concentrated on his point. If Michael could do what he wanted, that was all that concerned Horace G. Plumer. He took all the subsequent displays of "temperament" (of which there were several) with the same imperturbability.

They were almost happy months for me. Hilda's brow smoothed, and she became interested in other matters again. I felt that my own personal hope of interesting her was becoming less futile. Plumer's oil seemed to have lubricated all the channels of our lives. I was able to go back to my work, which had been badly neglected, and to my old interests. It helped my self-respect that I had been the medium of this piece of good-fortune to Bristowe, and I did not mind that he showed little gratitude and still often treated me with offhand mockery. My confidence began to return. However much a man may have been battered, does he ever entirely lose faith in his "luck," his special destiny? I reflected that I had always somehow got through my difficulties before. I had been foolish to imagine this difficulty insuperable. That article of mine—it might look like a fluke—but, from a more intelligent point of view, wasn't it just the triumph of experience and determination? A man of intellect, I told myself, will always find some way out of any complication if he keeps on trying long enough.

If Michael Bristowe's special capacity became acknowledged, if he acquired a stable standing through his success in this commercial enterprise—and there seemed to be nothing to prevent it—his dependence upon Hilda would cease and he would pass naturally into other spheres. Already they were seeing less of each other, owing to Michael's absorption in his experiments. Hilda, the task that she had set herself accomplished, would return to a more normal existence, to the social life that was natural to her and the ordinary pursuits of cultured people.

At first, I was dismayed when I found that she was to have a belated holiday early in the New Year, and meant to join her aunt for a month in her village on the Italian Riviera. Then it occurred to me that I might very well arrange to make a motor tour along the Riviera myself, if I left a decent interval after her departure. In Italy I should be at home; I should be able to "show her round." Her aunt would be helpful. Out there, in the sunshine, away from London and Michael Bristowe and the associations of the past year, who could say what might not happen?

X

A FEW DAYS BEFORE THAT ON WHICH I HAD ARRANGED to start on the journey that was to lead me along the white road beside the bluest of blue seas to the little coast village where Hilda was sunning her Northern fairness, a dirty crumpled note in an uneducated hand was brought in to me as I sat at breakfast. It said briefly that Mr. Bristowe had been very ill for the last three days, and that, as Miss Torrington had left my address with the writer, "in case anything went wrong," she had taken the liberty of letting me know about it.

Hilda had asked me before she left not to lose sight of Michael, and I had given her my promise. I had accordingly been round once to his unattractive "rooms"—that is, his one dark ground-floor bed-sitting-room—but found him so deeply engrossed in his odd-looking magnetic apparatus that he had hardly a word to say to me. He had moved a switch, and asked me if I noticed any difference, and then when I had to say that I did not, and still said so after he had poured a little water into one of the metal receptacles, he had turned away from me with a gesture of hand and head such as I once saw a famous painter make when a girl told him that one of his pictures was "very pretty." It is not a manner of treatment that I am accustomed to provoke, and, though I had learnt by this time to allow for Bristowe's peculiarities, I thought he owed me more politeness, and did not prolong my visit. I had not meant to go back there again before I left; the boy was obviously all right, and occupying himself after his own fashion. It could not be long now before he heard from Plumer, and then his future would be assured.

I took it that he now had an attack of 'flu. The weather had been vile during the last week, snow showers followed by quick thaws, and there was the usual spring epidemic. I went round to him later in the morning in some impatience, but without serious misgiving.

Michael's slatternly landlady, a compromise between the genteel, if hard-faced, dames of Bloomsbury and the unpretentious lodging-house keepers of Islington, between whom she lay geographically, met me with a face of melancholy importance. I had seen her before, and I noticed that she regarded my appearance with that lower-middle-class mingling of secret gratification and the determination to show that she thought herself "as good as I was," that always makes my gorge rise, so that I restrained with difficulty an impulse to walk away. I questioned her shortly about Michael.

He had been very ill indeed, she told me, with suppressed gusto, holding me in the passage, and added some unpleasant details. "It" had come on after he had gone out in a snowstorm without his coat at the beginning of the week. But he had been "queerish" even before that—she gave me a measuring side-glance. He had had a letter that same morning—he didn't often get letters—not lately; perhaps it might have been bad news.

I saw that she had got the letter in question, and wanted to be coaxed into sharing its contents. I said that Mr. Bristowe's correspondence did not interest me, and that I should like to see him. She told me that "the poor young man had been a bit light-headed and talking queer ever since last night, and that was why she had sent for me. It was very awkward to have illness in a house like hers—her other lodgers," etc., etc.

Finally, I pushed past her and entered the dark ground-floor room where Bristowe lived and slept. It was cold, yet airless, with a small smoky fire. Michael in the bed was in a high fever, and coughing incessantly.

There was no alternative but to take charge. I sent out for a doctor, who diagnosed pneumonia, and evidently considered the case serious. I paid heavily in advance to have a nurse accommodated on the premises, and to have the proper remedies provided for the patient.

Before I left I asked the woman for the letter which Michael had received on the day when his illness began. He was incapable of attending to his own business at present, and I told myself that there might be something urgent in it. My secret thought was that it might be from Hilda, though I could not conceive what she could write that would be likely to disturb Michael. But I meant to see it.

The old hag hesitated, nonplussed. She did not want to confess directly that she had it.

"Quickly, please. I'm in a hurry." I used a tone which always has its effect upon her kind, and with muttered grumbles and half apologies the letter came laboriously out of an under-pocket.

I stood a moment in the passage staring at it. It was not from Hilda. It was from Horace Plumer, and, as well as I can recollect, it ran as follows:

"Dear Mr. Bristowe,—

"You will have read in the papers of the great invention
of a 'Geological Camera' just announced by Professor
Shannon, by means of which photographs can be taken
of subterranean strata. My syndicate proposes to invest in
one of these cameras which are shortly, we understand, to
be put on the market, and we have decided, therefore, not
to take up the option on your services which we secured
in November last."

The letter ended with the usual compliments, and remem-
brances to Miss Torrington and myself, with thanks for "our
very pleasant association."

There was no end to it. That was the first thought that
passed through my startled brain. We were back again exactly
where we had started. I caught the sound of Michael's raised
voice in the neighbouring room, and distinguished the word
"Hilda." As I glanced at the door behind which he lay, one of
those ideas that spring from the primitive savagery in all of us
passed through my mind. Remembering it, I am glad to think
that a man is not responsible for everything that occurs to
him—if we cannot now put the onus upon the Devil, we can
still put it upon that old half-ape who takes so much killing.
Nevertheless, I think I must have turned pale.

I was brought back to common-sense by the old crone who,
unable to restrain her curiosity, was edging nearer to peer into
my face.

"All right." I pocketed the letter. "I'll see to this."

I got away only by promising more money for "expenses,"
and found myself in the street.

I made for my club on foot, in an effort to reduce my mental disturbance, and tried to recall something about the "Geological Camera." I found I remembered it only as a recent heading in the papers, below which I had not troubled to read. The idea that it might have any possible bearing upon Bristowe's affairs and so, indirectly, upon my own, had never entered my head.

At the club, I had *The Times* file for the past fortnight brought to me, and found plenty of information on the subject. I cannot say that I made much of the scientific side of the new invention. Science according to the journalists has always seemed to me a particularly eggless omelette. But Professor Shannon's name was guarantee enough in itself that the eggs had actually been broken. As far as I could discover, the new "camera" consisted of a development of the X-ray principle, in which rays of other kinds were also used. By the various penetrating powers and the refraction of these the hidden composition of solid substances to a great depth could be detected. It was not so much a new discovery as an ingenious practical application of discoveries already made. The resulting "photographs," I gathered, would not be photographs in the ordinary sense at all (that was a journalistic simplification), but would, in fact, be more akin to spectra and would need expert interpretation. Professor Shannon, as with all his inventions, intended to make this new one readily accessible and as inexpensive as possible.

That was all that I could discover. But it was enough. If it could do what was claimed for it, it put Michael Bristowe and his chance-sent biological variation for all practical purposes hopelessly out of date. Humanity had another and more reliable (because mechanical) method of performing the same function. I wondered, in idle despair, what the philanthropic old scientist would have said if he could have known of this incidental result of his brilliant invention.

The misfortune was a heavy one. But I am afraid it was the fact that it was my misfortune as well as Bristowe's that weighed most heavily upon me. What would Hilda do? Would she see that the fight was lost? And, in either case, what would become of Michael? There was no solution that would not be calamitous in some respect. And I had no genuine hope that Hilda would abandon the losing battle. She did not dissociate herself so easily from anything that had once engaged her loyalty. At the very best, I was doomed to a further period of stagnation in the matter that was nearest to my heart.

I went back to Michael's rooms the next morning in a mood of rebellion. I hated the place, the mean street, the odour of stale food in the passage, the detestable landlady, the sordid little sick-room. The nurse, obviously disgusted with her surroundings, told me that the doctor had already paid his visit, and he wanted to know who it was that the patient kept asking for. If she were a relation or a "close friend" (the middle-aged nurse smirked a little), he thought she ought to be sent for. It might make a difference to the patient; he must be kept as quiet as possible. I replied by asking if there were any improvement. The nurse lifted her shoulders. No change was to be expected for a few days, "in any case."

Michael coughed and choked sickeningly on the bed, and then unexpectedly revived and looked at me with intelligence.

"Tell Hilda I want her," he said, before he relapsed into feverish mutterings again.

And so, once again, I was to be the instrument of my own frustration. If only I could have remained in ignorance of Michael's condition! In another two days I should have started; the note would probably never have caught me up. I should have reached Hilda in ignorance; she also would have been in ignorance. We should have had the perfect week that I had planned. But I did know, and nothing could annihilate the knowledge. So strong was my wish, that it seemed at that moment strange to me, an anomaly, that one could not decide to ignore a purely mental experience of one's own. But mere humanity constrained me. And then I remembered also that several other people knew now of my knowledge, and that, even if I had snatched my perfect week, it must have been at the price of losing Hilda for ever afterwards. Finally, I telegraphed to her without any palliation, "Michael seriously ill. Asking for you," and went to look up the arrivals of the next day's continental trains.

In the meantime, I interviewed Plumer. I did not expect anything from this, but it seemed to be the course indicated for the representative of Michael's interests. And, by this time, I had worked myself into a grim conscientiousness about all that concerned Michael's interests.

It was odd to see the little jerky figure of Plumer again in the light of disillusionment. Our guardian angel, our sun from the West, who had magically cleared the fog of misunderstanding, and lit up all the future before us, was just a little, common, commercial American now, in the cold light of that garish hotel sitting-room where he granted me a hasty interview. He was platitudinously practical, and I saw now that that cutting, untrammelled intelligence of his, which had commanded my reluctant admiration, was merely an axe with which to hew out the directest path possible to the "almighty dollar." Intelligence without wisdom—never at any other time have I fallen under its cheap fascination! Nor do I think that anything less than the base stupidity which had involved us, like weeds clinging about a swimmer's legs, in that odious Press fracas, could have made me see it as a sun of enlightenment. At any rate, the glamour was gone now.

After his kind, Plumer behaved with perfect correctness, and even indulgence. He was evidently surprised to see me, though amiable as ever. I explained to him something of the effect of his repudiation of Michael Bristowe. Clearly, he did not see how the matter concerned him—it was the Fortune of Commerce. After all, he pointed out, our side had got £200 for nothing out of it. He wasn't squealing about that. Neither had we anything to squeal about. Young Bristowe had a very remarkable faculty—most *re*markable—but surely we saw that its market value had gone with the new invention? No one but a durned fool would take on a man for a purpose of this sort, when he could get an absolutely safe and reliable scientific process like Shannon's, and probably for a less outlay. A man might fail them, or go sick, or die, or throw them over. But he needn't tell *me* all that. He advised me to put Michael to a trade as soon as he was well again. He'd never make anything of the other thing now. Tough for him, of course, but he was young enough. He'd better forget it and put his mind to something that had dollars in it. I'd be sure to give his respects to Miss Torrington, wouldn't I? A real English lady—"one of the finest things God ever made."

X I

MICHAEL BRISTOWE'S ILLNESS WAS A LONG ONE, AND one that relinquished its victim slowly and reluctantly, retreating as for a fresh spring. I do not think he would have lived through it at all, if it had not been for Hilda. Perhaps it would have been better for him and for everyone concerned if he had not lived through it; certainly, it would have been better for me. But Hilda was determined that he should live, and he did live.

He came back to life an invalid with a weak chest which needed constant watchfulness, and a fretful neurasthenic of intolerable whims and moodiness. The up-grade phases of high spirits which had alternated with his periods of depression never occurred now; the spring of the reaction seemed to be broken; his mood hardly left one dead level of sullenness and dejection. By the time he was convalescent, his face had assumed the drawn-down look of the confirmed melancholic.

And Hilda, too, altered. She quickly lost the fresh bloom of her curtailed holiday, and that sternness which had begun to harden her young face ever since Selver's treachery became more pronounced. When I had shown her the American's letter and described my interview with him, she had said very little, as was usual with her in moments of disappointment. What she said concerned Michael's situation only:

"I ought to have been here."

I began to protest.

"No," she stopped me. "I'm not blaming myself, Ralph. I couldn't possibly have foreseen anything like this. But it is a great misfortune that I was not here… And then it snowed that same morning."

"Snowed?… Oh, you mean Michael's going out in it? He needn't have played that fool's trick, certainly."

"Snow is an intoxication to him," said Hilda. "It is the beauty of the crystals. He can't resist it. I can see exactly how it was. He would dash out into it that morning after getting this letter, just as another man might gulp raw whisky."

So that crazy action also was a by-product of Bristowe's incalculable singularity. One never knew where it would break out next. It was like high explosive, and we were like children playing with it. It frightened me nowadays to remember that Hilda had deliberately helped to develop it, so that its potentialities had become infinitely greater than they ever need have been. And now also, as I soon began to realise, the personality that controlled them was more irresponsible than ever.

The first time I saw Bristowe after he had begun to recover, Hilda stopped me quietly outside the door of the sick-room and made me take all the coins out of my pockets and leave them in my overcoat in the hall.

"He can't stand the alloy in them," she told me. "He says it's like having a Klaxon in the room."

"Dear me! Is that going to be permanent? Rather awkward, later on, won't it be?" I was flippant over a misgiving and a sense of indignity, as I emptied my pockets obediently.

Hilda answered me: "Oh no, I don't suppose so. It is just until he is better. These things seem to affect him more now, just as noises irritate ordinary people more when they are ill."

But I could see that she also was uneasy.

"He puzzles the doctor," she continued, with an attempt at a smile, "though he won't accept our explanation for a moment. He thinks Michael *hears* the coins in one's pocket. He says it's a remarkable case of hyperacousia in convalescence, and that we must try to reduce it."

I wondered whether one ought not indeed to wish that medical science could reduce it, could abolish it altogether, and throw back into the faces of the gods their fatal gift to Michael Bristowe. For, to this point of view I had now passed. I had been scornful at first in my thoughts of Horace Plumer, but, after all, he represented the world, the thing that is, not only America, but the rest of us also. In America it is merely more clear-cut and open. I saw that I had been partially hypnotised into sharing Hilda's view of Michael's gift. Now I was swinging back to a more practical position. After all, as the world is constituted, the value of everything depends ultimately on its use to society. Seer, saint, superman, whatever we may be, if we can do nothing in this relation, we are of no avail. And what one can do depends, not only on intrinsic possibilities, but on what one can get the opportunity to do. People were crudely right; their attitude to Michael Bristowe was right. He might have the most magnificent and unique knowledge and experience, but if he could find no way of translating them into terms of life, into what, whether we like it or not, is now measured by "exchange value," they went for nothing. His gift was useless now, superseded for every imaginable practical purpose by Professor Shannon's invention;

and he was no more than an ailing penniless youth, without
work or prospects, and cursed with a repellent and intractable
disposition.

At the time I said nothing of this to Hilda, for an irritable
voice hailed us from the room:

"Can't you come in and stop whispering there?"

It was a fortnight later that Hilda took him down to my house in
Dorsetshire. It was all very reasonable, and it was like a fatality.
Bristowe had to be got away to a milder climate, and he was
not fit to journey abroad. The notice was too short for Hilda's
old friends, the Naylors, with whom he had stayed before, their
rooms being already occupied; and, in any case, I guessed that
both Michael and Hilda were short of money by this time.
Michael, of course, would have spent the £200 he had had
from Plumer—I felt sure enough of that. And the expenses of
his illness, of which I had paid only the initial ones, must have
taxed Hilda's resources. She knew that I had kept Marling open
in charge of a housekeeper since my mother's death, though
I went down there very seldom; so that when, with her usual
frank confidence that I was as anxious as herself for Michael's
welfare, she asked me to let them use the place for a few weeks,
it was impossible for me to refuse. Besides, I reflected that the
presence of Mrs. Marshall, who was an impoverished gentle-
woman, one of my mother's protégées, would at least save the
proprieties, which they might very well ignore if they went
elsewhere. Moreover, the situation would remain within my
purview, if not under my control, and I could go down myself
if I wished. It was bitter-sweet to know that Hilda would be
under my roof in these conditions, and, even if I went, it would

be a miserable substitute for the Riviera holiday. But I knew well enough that I should go, none the less.

I did not ask Hilda what she had arranged about her own work in the meantime. Evidently that was to go to the wall. It had been a sufficient reason for refusing to consider marriage with me; it apparently had no weight against the necessity for nursing Michael Bristowe. I learnt, however, that Mrs. Hastings was keeping her post open for her. It was evident that Hilda was now drawing for Michael not only upon her actual account at the bank, but upon the fund of credit represented by her past usefulness to her employer.

I kept away until they had been at Marling for a week, and then sent a wire and went down, half shuddering at the pain that I knew I should experience, half hopeful that, after all, some advantage might come to me from the situation. But I found that I had hardly realised the nature or strength of the ordeal to which I had voluntarily subjected myself.

For to see Hilda at Marling was purgatory. I had never understood before how far my early sentiment for her had been bound up with my sentiment for my beautiful old home. My mother had been an artist in the art of living—an artist of an old school—of that gracious, well-ordered, country-house life of England, which, perhaps, like other modes of life, like Paganism and Chivalry, never approached its ideal perfection until its day was already passing. It was a part of my mother's artistry that she had seen Hilda as the future mistress of Marling. And I, too, had seen and loved Hilda in that sense. I began to understand why, though I loved the place, I had cared to visit it so little since it had become exclusively my own, while yet some obscure impulse had made me keep it open and ready for habitation at any moment.

Now, when I saw her at that first moment of my arrival, coming down the noble wide stairway into the old hall, her hair gleaming in the soft lights, it was as if an ideal picture had come to life. There are forms of modern life that kill the beauty of an old country house—a species of murder that I have often had to watch—giggling flappers, guffawing youths, shrill-voiced Americans, rowdy children whose proper milieu is the slum pavement. Blatant, miscellaneous, meaningless, they take advantage of their little vivacious moment of organic existence to annihilate the exquisiteness of the old walls that have absorbed all that was dignified in the humanity of past centuries and rejected all that was trivial and ephemeral. But Hilda's young dignity was the form of youth and life that fulfilled them, gave them their latest expression. As she moved to meet me, she seemed as perfectly in place as the Princess of Thule, whom I had always chosen to imagine her ancestress, bestowing gifts in her father's high hall.

Marling brought back this old conception of Hilda. And it did not clash with it, but rather gave it a new meaning and pathos that I knew her now also, and loved her as an individual. I knew her intimately now; I knew even what seemed to me her defects, but I knew nothing cheap or small. Even for her young hardness, even for her limitations, it seemed to me now that I loved her helplessly the more. I loved her even the more for the pain that she had caused me. It seemed to commit me spiritually, as capital poured into an enterprise commits one to see it through—if it fails, too much will be lost, more than will bear thinking of. Yet I had not been able to win her, and I was beginning seriously to wonder if I ever should.

I was grateful afterwards for that first hour that I had Hilda to myself. It was an hour near to happiness. I had arrived a little late for tea, but she had it brought, none the less, into the sunny little afternoon sitting-room, which looked out on to the garden of spring flowers. I asked after Michael, and she replied; but we did not talk much of him, and I did not ask where he was. We were both exiles returned to our native country-side, and the soft clear air of that exquisite spring evening was intoxicating to us. We talked of old times, of my mother, of other people we had both known and of their present fortunes. We mourned together that Hilda's old home was in pawn to a profiteer. In such a conversation, even woes take on a pleasurable colour.

And then Michael came. As always, Michael intruded. And this time he did not even come himself. A word from him, sent through Mrs. Marshall, a peremptory gesture, and my good hour was over.

"Mr. Bristowe says will you go to him in the library now, Miss Torrington? He says he must get that machine in order, if he is to use it to-night... I kept him lying down as long as I could." The good lady was addressing Hilda, but had not the tact to refrain from a deprecatory glance at me. She knew, of course, all about that old family plot.

Perhaps her attitude affected Hilda, for Hilda also seemed for once vaguely aware of my indignation.

"Tell him I will come," she said; and turned to explain to me that she had had Michael's magnetic apparatus put in the library. "I'm trying to get him to take an interest in it again," she said; "it seems the only thing that has the remotest chance of interesting him." The trouble stood plain to be seen in her eyes. "I asked old Naylor to come in to-night, so that Michael could try him with it."

So the old "dowser" also was now to be drawn into Michael's weird experiments. The idea interested me, in spite of my vexation, and I sat thinking it over for a few moments when she had left me. From one point of view it was an intelligent move on Hilda's part. One of our problems in dealing with Michael had always been that we had too little check upon him. How can blind men check the claims of the only one among them who sees? He got results, we had been compelled to admit that, with all that it implied; but there had been no one so far who could even question him intelligently about his methods. This old man, who presumably shared his faculty to however small a degree, and would therefore have some inkling of what it signified, would be a crucial witness. So much for the abstract scientific side. But, again, it was another push ahead into the unknown regions of the new thing, and I had definitely decided now that we had already gone too far. Professor Shannon's invention had destroyed the significance of the enterprise, had left us in the air. I was convinced by this time that it would be better—and not only for my own private interests, but for Michael himself and, above all, for Hilda—to let the matter rest and trouble about it no more. Michael might in time lose again something of his abnormality: it had certainly been sharpened by exercise, it might become dulled again by judicious neglect. He might yet find some *modus vivendi* as an ordinary man among ordinary men. Anyhow (for my mind, after all, misgave me, as I thought of his ravaged face), we could do our best to give him the chance, and the result would not be our responsibility.

And then Hilda added to my misgiving by slipping out of the library to me as I went to dress. She spoke in a deprecating, half-worried whisper, unlike herself. "Coins still worry Michael, Ralph… If you wouldn't mind…" I nodded and turned away, sick at heart.

When I met him at dinner, the impression was confirmed yet further. It seemed to me that I had been distressing myself about his future unnecessarily. He so plainly had no future. It was the first time that I had seen him out of bed since his illness. It was not so much that he still looked a physical wreck. A more essential vitality had gone out of him. I had seen a similar thing before, more than once—I suppose that everyone over thirty must have seen it—one or two men who had failed in their professions in those devastating post-war years; one who was doing well enough, but had made the wrong marriage; an older family friend, bright-eyed and vigorous before the War, who had lost both his sons at Ypres. Something is gone, the snap, the power of reaction; they are all men without futures. It matters no longer what may happen to them.

The contrast was the greater in Bristowe, in that there had always been that peculiar suggestion of potential energy in him, more personality, I suppose one must call it, than most people possess. I had been consciously dreading his clash with the atmosphere of Marling, and squaring myself for it. I had expected, remembering that savage suppressed vitality of his, that he would kill it as completely as any shrieking flapper or grotesque ex-grocer. It would not, I had admitted, be the same sort of clash as that of the parvenu or the degenerate, but a finer affair—more like a duel, less like a butchery, but none the less effectual for that.

I found now that my fears had been quite unnecessary. This sullen apathetic creature was obviously incapable of putting up a fight of any sort. Even our good Burgundy roused him only to a kind of dull malice, a poor shadow of his old mischievousness, though even more exasperating.

I think the source of the trouble must have been that, innocently enough, I had dressed for dinner. It would have been impossible for me not to do so this first evening that I entertained Hilda in my own house, even if I had thought of the probability that Michael would not possess a dress-suit; but, in fact, no speculation on the point had entered my head. Michael said nothing directly on the subject, but I had caught more than one unpleasant glance at my expanse of shirt-front. He himself was in an old lounge suit, though Hilda had changed into a simple evening dress. He began by remarking with an almost open sneer, half-way through the somewhat silent meal, that he had never lived in a house half the size of Marling before, and continued with a series of the sort of remark by which members of the lower middle class commonly try to demonstrate themselves completely at ease in circumstances that, in fact, overawe them. He tried to be jocular in a mumbling sort of way about the one man-servant whom I had retained, about the number of bathrooms, about people who dined in the evening. I found it difficult to reply with bare civility. Even in his most objectionable moments, that strange hint about him of a hidden demoniac energy had always redeemed him from vulgarity. This evening he seemed merely the gauche, half-educated, bourgeois youth eating with his betters, and trying to bolster up his self-respect with half-spiteful, half-servile chaff. I looked at Hilda to see how she was taking this exhibition, but she was sitting with quiet introspective eyes, evidently musing over something. Only once her glance rested thoughtfully on Michael.

"You're tired, Michael," she said. "Shall I put Naylor off till another evening?"

"I'm always tired," Michael snapped suddenly. "It might as well be this evening as any other." And then, to my relief, he became silent.

XII

I TAKE AGAIN A NEW PAGE AND MAKE A NEW START,—I
hardly know why, since this is not a formal narrative, but a
sequence of experience in reminiscence. And yet one's memory,
dwelling upon the past, instinctively divides it into parts—into
chapters, into sections, into paragraphs, corresponding to the
unities of experience, to the rises and falls of the intensity of
consciousness. Every night closes a chapter, and every morning begins a new one; yet there are also chapters shorter than
a day in one's life—hours and half-hours of heightened living,
cut off before and after by flat stretches which are relatively of
no greater significance than the hours spent in sleep.

And the hour we spent in the library at Marling that evening was, to me at least, an experience so much apart as to be
almost on a plane of existence other than that of ordinary life. It
seemed as much of its own kind as the experience of watching
the acting of a tragedy. And if it had, in fact, been rounded off
like a stage play, without practical implications, and had affected
my life no more than the actions of the imaginary characters
of "Hamlet" or "Œdipus" affect one's life the next morning, it
would have been very well for me. But how is one to deal with
a Hamlet who, as a child would say, "comes real"?

The evening certainly began in no impressive manner.
Hilda and Michael went to the library immediately dinner was
over, and a few minutes later the old farmer, Naylor, arrived.

I welcomed the splendid old man with relief after my conflict with Michael's manner at dinner. Like most of the old yeomen stock, Naylor was one who "knew his place" and graced it.

I sent him on to join them in the library, and, after a moment, made up my mind to follow. A man may be unwelcome in his own library, but he can hardly be turned from the door.

I saw at once that, in the short interval, Michael had somehow managed to work himself into a state of meaningless hysterical exasperation. He refused to begin making the tests with his apparatus, though the old man, invited for the purpose, was quietly waiting.

"Oh, what's the use of bothering? He won't feel anything." Although he had had no possible cause for annoyance, Michael spoke in the strained dangerous voice of one who is utterly at the limits of his patience. He had thrown himself into one of the leather arm-chairs in a queer twisted attitude, with hanging arm and head, sagging in the middle. He was apt, as I had often noticed before, to adopt such postures—the sort of posture which I have always despised in the modern "artistic" youth.

Hilda bent over him, talking quietly, while Naylor stood waiting with a perfect reticent dignity. I walked away, unwilling to be drawn in, and glanced over the odd mechanism on the table. I had seen it before, of course. It was a queer untidy-looking object—a miscellany of batteries, stands and small magnets all connected up in various ways with a switchboard of numbered switches. It looked complicated and unintelligible, but was, in fact, merely a cumbrous way of doing a very simple thing, or rather a number of simple things—that is, of sending magnetic currents through various kinds of metals, separately, or at the same time. The switches formed a rough sort of keyboard by which these combinations were controlled. I do not think that Michael can have had much mechanical talent; there was nothing about the machine of the trimness which one sometimes sees in the apparatus set up by quite young boys. Probably a smart boy of fourteen could have made it very much better for him, if he could have explained what he wanted. But then, probably, no mechanic, boy or man, could have understood what he wanted, or why he should want it. It must have been a strong impulse, I thought, that had made him undertake so uncongenial an effort. Even to me, who am myself nothing of a mechanic, the thing looked pathetic in its clumsiness, like the stone axe-heads of primitive man.

"Well, if you won't, Michael, I shall." Hilda's firm voice broke in upon my reflections. She stepped up beside me, and began moving the switches in a haphazard manner.

Michael sprang to his feet with a furious exclamation. A sudden influx of energy seemed to fill his limp figure as he almost hurled himself across the floor towards us.

"For God's sake, Hilda, leave that alone!" He pushed her roughly to one side, and snapped off again the switches she had moved.

It was the first time I had ever known him rude to Hilda, in spite of his frequent incivilities to other people, and my temper blazed. I started forward, and should have taken him by the collar if Hilda's hand had not fallen compellingly on my arm.

"The point is,"—she turned to where the quiet old man was still standing—"did Naylor notice anything?"

"Well, miss," he answered deprecatingly, "I did seem to see a sort of a light."

"A light!" Michael, suddenly struck quiet, gazed at him with bent brows for a moment. Then he woke to an abrupt, business-like activity. "Look here, sit down there." He put Naylor into a chair, a little way in front of the apparatus, made him extend his hands on his knees, and stepped back to the switchboard.

Hilda gently drew me away to one of the window seats. Dusk was just falling outside, and the light in the room was getting dim. Once I moved to put on the lights, but Hilda's hand restrained me as she whispered in my ear that Michael preferred to be without them. The scene began to take on a fantastic quality. Ignored, outsiders, we watched, for what seemed hours, a process which we were incapable of comprehending. Only occasional odd snatches of conversation, a quick question and answer, exclamations, told us that things were happening, things of which we had no cognisance, as Michael moved his switches up and down.

"How's that?"

"It's a sort of a blue flame, Mr. Michael... oh!... you're spoiling it!"

"Shut your eyes," Michael commanded abruptly, and the old man obeyed. Some more manœuvres followed.

"Now. That's not a flame, is it?"

"No... It's something different. It's like a flame, but it isn't... I don't know how to say it."

Something between a chuckle and a grunt came from Michael. "Never mind. Don't try," he said. "There aren't any words for it. If you know the difference, that's all I want."

It was like hearing a man communicate with invisible spirits. The strangeness of it was almost intolerable. My mouth went dry, and I felt my hair lift as I watched. Michael's isolated feats had never affected me as powerfully as this. In our presence, under our eyes, waves were passing, communications effected, understandings attained, while for us absolutely nothing was happening. That was what terrified—not that for them something happened, but that for us there was nothing. I have heard "the direct voice" at a spiritualist séance, but it never gave me so eerie a sensation as this. I strained all my senses, I held all my muscles rigid, I made myself into a quivering receptivity. And there was nothing, absolutely nothing.

In an attempt to keep my mental balance, I tried to rationalise the thing. Evidently the sequence of Michael's currents signified something, both to himself and to Naylor. There must be some kind of rhythm, some principle of harmony, implied. It occurred to me that the only normally constituted man who might begin to understand it would be a mathematician. He might perhaps have found some remote, abstract, harmonic law in Michael's combinations, and formed some idea of them on that plane of pure intellect of which most of us can hardly even realise the existence. Even this suggestion of explanation seemed to comfort me a little. Then I started violently as Naylor shifted in his seat and gave an uneasy grunt.

"All right. I'll stop it." Michael looked up at him, and, as in the old days before his illness, I saw the broad elfish grin light up his dark face.

I glanced at Hilda. She was flushed and taut, her eyes travelling from the alert figure of Michael to the old man in his chair. It was clear that for her, as for me, the only drama that was passing was what we could see dimly reflected in our companions' faces.

And then, suddenly, after a few moments' silence, Naylor's face, on which my eyes were fixed, seemed to wrinkle and break up, so that I drew in a sharp breath. The next moment he had broken into a clear gentle laugh of such pure quality of amusement as I have heard from a musical child at the finish of one of Grieg's goblin pieces. And, as he heard it, Michael threw up his head and laughed too, pleasantly, like a child.

I think it was that laugh that completed my demoralisation. It was as if we were "fairy-led." I have no very clear idea of what followed. All those monsters of the mind which one's consciousness ordinarily keeps at bay came swarming over the border. Reality had become vague and wavering; the bounds of personality were moved. I no longer felt sure if this were indeed my own library at Marling or some unsubstantial circumstance called up from a dream world. In the growing darkness, lit only by the flickering of the fire, Michael at his machine seemed half wizard, half monster, and the white-bearded old man on the chair seemed to advance and recede, to swell and to shrink, as if he had been a demon inadequately materialised from another plane of existence. I know that Michael went on for a long time, moving those flexible white hands of his over the switches, and I was conscious that abrupt questions and answers were still passing, and that Michael muttered frantically from time to time, "But that's nothing! That's nothing!" and then went on again. But I was engrossed with the fragmentary ideas flung out by the turmoil of my own mind. Only Hilda, sitting beside me, with shining watchful eyes, seemed to retain full reality. I fixed my eyes on her face as on the only stable refuge in a tottering world.

"It's very clumsy. There's an awful lot to do yet. I shall never finish it; but I'll do better than this." Michael's voice, perfectly matter-of-fact, but alert and vigorous, as I had not heard it since his illness, cut through my dazzlement. And I heard old Naylor's reply.

"It's wonderful, Mr. Michael, it's wonderful. I don't rightly understand it all—you mustn't think that I do. But it's wonderful, I can see that... I can't say what I mean as I'd like to..." They were standing together by the door.

"No one can say anything about this..."

I realised that they had finished and were going, but I could not summon the energy to move.

Hilda, too, sat on for a moment.

"They've forgotten us," she said at last, and drew herself to her feet with a difficult effort. "I must go after them. Michael will be worn out... He'll be needing me."

Left by myself, I came back slowly to normality. Presently, I was ashamed and distressed to find that tears were running down my face. I do not know whether it is truly a disgrace to a man to recognise an utterly new thing with a flood of tears. But this new thing was my enemy, and I did not know how to fight it. Michael's faculty, a nuisance, a marvel, a puzzle, many things before that day, had suddenly become a live menacing entity in a sense that it had never been before. It was partly that another man had recognised it, however imperfectly. It had proved itself communicable; that seemed to give it a validity it had never yet possessed. But my state of shock was due also to the realisation that it had creative force. I knew intuitively, with the knowledge that belongs to one who has himself, however meagrely, the power of creation, that what I had been present at that evening had been an artistic achievement. I had been present at it—not witnessed it, not listened to it—for this was art beyond my range, art in a sphere to which I had no access. The humiliation had to be accepted. And Michael—the tiresome insufferable neurasthenic—had greatness because of it. He had greatness as a man of genius has it, who may be intolerable in himself, yet is the vehicle of something transcendent.

As I forced myself to think more quietly, I began to apply what I had observed to be Hilda's method in dealing with Michael's peculiarity—to work out an analogy with the senses that we know. I considered, was the boy then an artist? He had, of course, the "artistic temperament," as it is commonly recognised, but which, in fact, often exists apart from any creative skill. How were we to know whether he was an artist in this unique sphere of his, where, at best, there could be hardly any who could begin to follow him at an immense distance, and no one who could criticise? We had only old Naylor's testimony that Michael's inexplicable vagaries with his magnets had indeed produced something significant, something with the principle of symmetry in it. It might be comparable to "Jack and Jill," or to "Paradise Lost"; it might be a jazz jingle or a Moonlight Sonata.

Then I realised that such absolute pioneer work could hardly be measurable on any such scale. It would be more analogous to the scratchings of a mammoth or a buffalo made by a man of the Stone Age on a tusk—those drawings where power and spirit strove so heroically through the poverty of the instruments, or to the first rhythmic beating of a tom-tom waking new delights in the breasts of a savage tribe. But these things were all relative, and we had no standard.

Speculation was useless... I longed with intensity to be rid of the whole coil. There was no way of tackling it. Why had this thing come upon me of all people upon earth? I was just a normal man who wanted the ordinary pleasant life of my country and my birth. I wanted Hilda, my natural mate, with whom I could share a happy and normal life. I did not expect to be proof against ordinary misfortune, or wish to shirk the usual responsibilities. I had gone voluntarily into the War at its beginning, and would have stayed it out without faltering, however long it had lasted… But this thing was not in the rules of the game of life, as I knew it. I felt that Fate had given me a foul blow; and I had a moment of sheer stupid rebellion against fact, such as I have always regarded as unworthy of a man of my race and class. I suppose that the long psychological struggle of the past year, with this incalculable factor in it, against which it was useless to fight, had undermined my manhood. For those few moments I couldn't help whining that "It wasn't fair!"

Just under the open window by which I was sitting, I heard Hilda letting the old farmer out at a little side door, and thanking him for his help to Michael.

The old man's voice, still clear and strong for all his years, but now with a quiver of pleading emotion in it, came up to me. "Look after him well now, Miss Hilda. There aren't many of his kind."

There was a moment's pause before Hilda answered. "None at all, I think… I mean to do everything that I can."

I shrank back into my seat, and thought seemed to stop as a black depression struck me like a sandbag.

XIII

I T IS STRANGE, AND IT MAY SOMETIMES BE TRAGIC, HOW unquestioningly one tends to accept the statements of other people. I mean more particularly statements of what they think and feel and intend. I am not, of course, referring to habitual poseurs, who are easily detected by any normal intelligence, but to the ordinarily straightforward person voicing his ideas about himself. Every man, looking into his own soul, knows himself to be a creature of complex personality, constantly changing in his views and desires, utterly unreliable, making statements with all possible variations from, and approxima- tions to, the truth, frequently deceiving even himself. This is a commonplace, and yet, I think, every man unconsciously assumes that other people's assertions have a stability that his own have not. I have often been appalled at the absolute faith with which people have accepted what I have told them of myself. Yet I realise that I continue to believe with a child-like naïveté, whatever they themselves may say.

Ever since Hilda had told me so positively on that first occasion at the Club, when I had remonstrated with her about her relations with Michael Bristowe, that she had no intention of marrying him, the thought of that particular danger had dropped completely from my mind. I knew that her sincer- ity was beyond question, and therefore her words seemed finally to settle the point. Quite unjustifiably, I had taken it as a permanent guarantee that no such question could ever arise between her and Michael, at any rate on her side. And I was the more secure in my assumption that my own observation told me that sex sensibility had never yet been aroused in her. Michael, or rather Michael's gift, I had certainly regarded as my rival, but merely as the pervading interest in Hilda's mind cutting across my own, and likely to delay the realisation of my hope indefinitely, or even, by unhappy chance, to vitiate my opportunity altogether.

And yet I cannot in honesty accuse Hilda of misleading me. I see now that the assertion on which I had been relying had long become out of date. Circumstances had altered enormously. Most probably, she had forgotten that emphatic assurance of nearly two years ago. Certainly, she could not have attached to it the importance that I had.

She came to me as I was walking in the garden that morning after the experiment in the library, unreasoningly cheered again after my night's depression by the beauty of the day and the momentary pleasantness of existence. The strain of the evening had been too great for Michael, and he had not been down to breakfast. Hilda had told me that she thought he would have to spend the day in bed, and I was well pleased to be spared his presence.

She fell into step beside me, and told me at once with a brave, full look, "Ralph, I have decided to marry Michael."

I was so completely unprepared that the statement had a stunning physical effect. I stopped in my walk, and must, I think, have staggered a little, for she seized my arm and looked at me anxiously. I remember that, but I do not clearly remember the moments that followed, until I found myself again walking forward beside her, exclaiming absurdly over and over, "You can't! You can't! You can't!"

Hilda walked beside me in silence a moment. Then she broke out:

"Oh, Ralph, I don't want to hurt you. It's just that I know that it's my job."

"Your *job*?"

"Michael wants me to marry him now. He never bothered about it before his illness—he was too much interested in what he was doing. But now he's afraid. He says he can't go and live alone again. He wants me there all the time."

"You don't love him?... But I know you don't. You couldn't."

Hilda hesitated. "No. I don't suppose so. He's been my strongest interest for a long time. You know that. But I've never been in love in the way people talk about it and the way books describe it. I think, that I am probably not capable of that. You see, that makes this simpler for me."

"Simpler!" I spoke with a savage brutality which only the violence of the shock I had received could excuse. "Do you know what you are talking about?... Look here, Hilda, you are not an early-Victorian. You must have some idea what marriage means."

"Of course I know, Ralph." She answered me a trifle impatiently, but added in a lower tone after a moment: "And if you think I am doing this quite easily..."

A wave of mingled relief and anger passed through me at the implied admission. "Then why, my dear girl, why, in God's name...?"

She answered my uncompleted question in a low tone, after a moment. "You saw last night, Ralph. You were there. That is

what has finally decided me. You know that Michael is different
from anyone else—that he's more important. If *he* goes under,
humanity may lose a chance that may never come again... And I
am the only person who can do anything. He wants me to marry
him, and I don't believe he would ever marry anyone else...
And his health is in a very bad state. He couldn't stand another
attack—the doctor warned me... It depends on me, Ralph."

I reflected bitterly that Michael, like more commonplace
men, was evidently employing the strike method. Many of my
acquaintances have got themselves married after that fashion. It
may vary in intensity from the "My life is ruined—I shall go to
the dogs" whine to the unashamedly suicidal type. Here, too,
people, and more especially women, believe too easily.

Hilda was going on, defending her impossible case. "Then,
there's the money question, too. Michael doesn't think about
that. But I have to. He's only got his tiny income. He can't live
on that; but, if we are together, we can live on what I have and
what I can earn. I'm afraid London's become impossible for
Michael. It was getting very bad even before he was ill... There
are too many things there—too much confusion... And then
this business of the coins—and other things, too, that you don't
know about... But now we shall be able to take a country cottage somewhere, on the Downs, perhaps, and I can go up to
Town every day. We can manage, if we are careful."

It was horrible to me to hear her planning like this, as if
this nightmare notion were really to be accomplished—planning to pinch and struggle, counting up her resources, so that
she might support an idle and helpless husband. The sight of
some of my comrades of the War, easy-going generous fellows
when I had known them, now cheeseparing and worrying over

every halfpenny, obsessed by the mere effort to keep going the bodies of themselves and their dependents, deteriorating into wrinkled scarecrows, had sickened me many times since I had come home. It seemed another nightmare coming upon the first that I should be listening to Hilda talking in the same strain in my own garden, under the shadow of my own lovely home. But I could not use this as an argument with her.

"If he's such a crock as all that," I said at last, "what good do you think he can do, however much you help him?"

"I'm not expecting anything of Michael himself now. He's done for, Ralph." Her voice shook a little. "They've wrecked him, in spite of all that we could do… You haven't seen much of him since his illness. But I know. Last night was only a flash. He'll never really be good for anything again."

"But then—"

"But we may have a child, or children, you see, and they may inherit his gift from Michael. It's the only chance."

I was silent for a moment in complete stupefaction. It was almost incredible that an adult woman should speak to me in this manner about the supreme experience of her sex. And then I realised that, of course, it was because Hilda was not, emotionally, an adult woman that it was possible for her to do it. She was a child still—the precious child whom I loved and had to save, at all costs, from herself.

I tried roughness, as one might call harshly to a child straying near the edge of a precipice, though Heaven knows my heart was bleeding with love and fear.

"You are going to marry Michael Bristowe and have children by him in order that a superior strain of the human animal may not die out?"

She flushed a little, but more, I think, at my tone than at my words. She had never flinched in the face of facts; and she accepted my statement of the case now.

"Yes, Ralph," she said quietly. "Isn't it important enough?"

"Important? I don't know. I think sanity is more important... Why do people come of age at twenty-one? It ought to be thirty at the earliest. People in their twenties may do anything. One is saner at twelve."

Hilda said nothing, and I pulled myself up. I knew well enough that this was no way to deal with her. I should have to meet her on her own plane of reasoned thinking, and argue this preposterous question as a matter of logic and utility. I drove under my own desperation and faced the necessity. I would do even that if it would suffice to save her.

I began to question her as calmly as I could. I found quickly that what I was truly up against was a religion. It was a religion, young and hard, like Hilda herself, though so far as it had a name it was kin to the so-called "Religion of Humanity." Hilda had the modernist's vision of the universe evolving itself blindly from the chaos of matter, working itself up the scale through inorganic nature to the generation of life, through all forms of life, plant, animal, human, pushing forward into consciousness, towards power and understanding; unhelped by any god, yet with the principle of divinity implicit in its own struggle. Of course, I had had glimpses before of this philosophy of Hilda's. I had also had opportunities enough to realise that, for her, the distance between theory and action, so wide for most of us, was dangerously small. But how far this tendency might carry her I had never realised before.

"Then you think," I said painfully, adjusting my mind with effort to her outlook, "that Michael Bristowe fits into this scheme of yours, that he represents another push towards fuller consciousness and power, as you say?"

"Ralph, you've seen. Not as much as I have, but enough to show you. Michael has possibilities that no one else has—more than possibilities—realisations. He is on a different plane of understanding."

"And, it makes him so much happier, doesn't it?" I broke in. "If you've studied the course of evolution so thoroughly, Hilda, you must have heard something also of the variations that didn't come off—whole races of creatures destroyed by their own overdevelopment on certain lines—giant reptiles, toothed birds, plated fishes. Has it occurred to you that Michael's case may be parallel to these rather than to that of the first bird that took to the air, or the first ape with 'an opposable thumb'?"

"Yes, Ralph. I've thought of that possibility, too. It's quite true that Michael's an adventure at best—an adventure of the race."

I pushed on, encouraged.

"Isn't it possible that the human mind may not be equal to the burden of six senses? There's more than one thing about Michael that suggests it, isn't there?... Doesn't the mere fact that he can't get on—can't find any practical use for his gift, can't fit into social relations—doesn't that really show that Nature can't do with him? That evolution is checking the development of the type he might give rise to?"

Hilda gave a mournful little laugh. "Ralph, my dear, don't drop into special pleading. You've seen it all along—this process of the checking. You must have seen that it represents nothing at all but a crazy confusion. Evolution has been in our hands, hasn't it, since we developed a social consciousness? But no one can say that we've made anything of it yet. We've muddled all the working of the old Survival of the Fittest agencies, and so far created nothing to take their place. Of course, it's impossible to know how Michael might have got on under primitive conditions, but it doesn't matter. Even if the human race couldn't have afforded such an expansion then, we may be able to afford it now—or we may be able to afford it a little later, if it can only be saved in the meantime. Only there is no co-operate intelligence to depend upon yet. Isn't that all the more reason why people who are conscious of these things, like you and me, should take care what they are about?"

"Well, take the case on its merits, then," I persisted. "Say that Michael's peculiarity would be transmitted—which is doubtful in itself—I don't see how it could be anything but a curse in modern life. You say he can't even stand London now. How do you suppose it would have been if he had been in the War, for instance? Five senses were too many there. Many a man went under from sheer sensual horror. Michael couldn't have stood a day of it... Why, you remember how he behaved when he discovered that murder... The development of this sense is positively dangerous in many ways."

"Yes, it's dangerous," said Hilda musingly, and by the little smile that moved her lips I saw, to my despair, that I had added an incentive against my cause. "Most adventures are dangerous... In that spirit one might wish to become deaf in order to sleep without being disturbed... Do you think that if you told

Michael he could become rich and influential and happy, if he would give up this extra perception of his, he would accept?... Besides, Ralph, my child would have a better chance than poor Michael has had. He wouldn't start with everything against him. It will be a fairer test."

The fresh allusion upset my poise. "And so you have made Michael Bristowe into a little tin Messiah who is going to raise the human race to higher things? I must say I prefer my Messiahs of a different type."

Hilda, as always, took the taunt and meditated upon it.

"I don't think I idealise Michael, Ralph," she said at last. "His gift is plain fact, isn't it? And so is my responsibility for him and it. I've been in it from the beginning, you know—it would never have reached this stage without me."

I groaned at the truth of that.

"As to the Messiah," she went on, "I suppose that's one way of putting it. Perhaps," her face seemed to take on a brooding pathos, "the Michael Bristowes are the only sort of Messiahs we can expect, now that we have lost our omnipotent God. Our God is one who needs our help. And it seems clear that this is my opportunity to help."

"Hilda, my dear, understand. No one really takes all that seriously. Not even the people who are most enthusiastic in preaching it. Not when it comes to one's personal life. Life isn't like that."

"If I take it seriously," said Hilda, slowly, "that will be one person at least, won't it?"

My exasperation broke through. "You don't think it may sound a little presumptuous to be so ready to take on responsibility for the whole human race?"

There was a pause.

"I am sorry that you think my ideas high-flown, Ralph," she said at last. "I have tried as hard as I can to be rational and practical about this."

"Rational! It's rationality that is the matter with you. Your generation seems to have imbibed Wells and Shaw with its mother's milk! I believe the *Peep of Day* was more wholesome!"

Hilda smiled a little sadly. "Don't forget the War, too, Ralph. Our third teacher."

"The War!... You talk as if I had not been in the War." I don't know why the childish impulse to say this took me. But Hilda answered me gravely.

"I know you were; very much more completely so than I was. But it wasn't the same thing. You were grown up when it started. All your ideas were formed already. I was still growing... It taught all of us who were young enough to learn that we had only ourselves to look to."

I left that. After all, the Religion of Humanity is as good as most religions so long as it is kept, as all religions should be, in its right place... After all, my attempt to argue the question had been insincere—I might have known that it would not avail me with Hilda. I did not, in fact, care whether Michael's gift would benefit the human race if it were preserved, or not. I cared that Hilda's life should not be spoilt. The difficulty was with her lack of the sense of proportion, with her immaturity in experience. I began to try to show her this, talking quietly, choosing my words with more care and pain than I have ever bestowed on the most literary of my essays. I tried, if human skill could do it, to draw her on to me, to show her something of what the years would show, to evade by some effort of spirit or twist of art the doom that one human being may not learn through the experience of another.

She listened to me patiently.

"You say that I shall grow out of this way of seeing things, Ralph," she answered me at last; "but are you sure that you don't mean *shrink* out of it? I can't deny that I may change, as you say. I think perhaps I can even dimly see how it might happen. I think you may be right, and that the impulse to do a thing of this sort may be a characteristic of youth. Does that really imply that it is less to be respected than the point of view that you say comes later? Mayn't it simply mean that one becomes more egoistic? You talk about experiences and disillusionments that will teach me what I really am, and what the world is, better than I can know it now. But how can I tell that they won't be actually more like a fog closing me in from what I now see clearly?"

"Hilda, my dear, wait anyhow until you have been in love— not with me, necessarily—with someone, anyone. You can't know what a horror marriage without love may be."

"I didn't think," said Hilda, though a sadness in her voice softened the mockery, "that I should ever hear you talk like a best-seller, Ralph... And it's only the other day that you were defending the French *mariage de convenance*."

It was true, of course. And I could not explain to her how it was that none of the many motives other than love that people may have for marrying—to obtain wealth or position, to escape from loneliness, or boredom, or humiliation—affected me with the same peculiar horror as this motive of hers—for the sake of an idea, a religion, in order to have a special kind of child. I could not explain to her because the horror was not rational, though I knew in the roots of my being that it was right.

She returned to the point a little impatiently. "I don't think I shall ever fall in love, Ralph. And Michael's affairs won't wait."

"You can't be sure that you will never fall in love," I persisted. "And you've no right to do this until you are sure... Don't you see how it is, my dear? There are some things that do violence to one's personality, that damage one beyond recovery. You yourself are the only instrument you have for the service of humanity or for anything else. If you do violence to that instrument, your capacity for service is ended."

I knew by the pause and change in Hilda's walk that this time I had reached her. This had come nearer to moving her than anything I had yet found to say. I waited in silence, almost holding my breath, afraid to add another word.

At last she said, speaking a little uncertainly, "Even that may happen, Ralph. I know there are all sorts of possible dangers. And nothing to guard one against danger. But still if I have done what is necessary before that, it may all the same be worth it... It's the only chance, you see, the one chance that Michael shall not have been quite useless, that he shan't have existed for nothing. So far as we can know, it's the one chance that a way of knowing and understanding shall not be closed to us for ever."

I lost my head. "Hilda, I beg you not to do this. It's wrong, it's horribly wrong for you. I know it. You must take my word for it. You will break my heart if you do it. It isn't because I want you for myself. You can leave me out of it. You need never see me again. But don't do this. It isn't a matter for argument. I can't argue with you. You've got a finer brain than I have..."

"Oh!" She began to laugh oddly, and I broke off, staring at her. "Don't, Ralph, my dear, don't. It's so horribly unlike you."

She half tumbled on to a seat near which we were passing, and the laughter became a burst of sobs. I had never seen her hysterical before; but I was myself too utterly exhausted to do anything but stare in a helpless agony. I knew that it was all over. This momentary nervous reaction did not mean that her resolution was wavering. This monstrous disaster was going to happen. I had put out all my strength, and I could not win. Hilda's own tough young strength was going to ruin her. I cannot recollect those moments even now without a sensation of sickness. The sudden collapse of all one's powers that follows too great a strain was upon me. Hilda quietened quickly, and, when she looked up again and begged me to go, I obeyed her without a word and dragged myself away like a half-shot rabbit struggling to its burrow.

XIV

I RETURNED TO LONDON THAT EVENING. ALL THE AFTER-
noon I had spent alone in my study, doing nothing, suffering the aftermath of my struggle with Hilda. I was abjectly
exhausted. Hilda's will set towards disaster was like an immov-
able barrier ahead. Yet for some time waves of thought continued to rise in me and surge and break against it. In the intervals,
I seemed to be a mass of aches—for I was at the point where
mental and physical suffering become indistinguishable—as
after a fall among rocks, when one has been bruised from head
to foot. In one of the moments when critical consciousness
detaches itself, I realised that I was adopting those same queer
postures, those hanging and sagging attitudes which I had
execrated in Michael Bristowe and in modern youth generally.
It came to me—an odd little scrap of psychological knowledge
salved among the wreckage—that they were, in truth, with
their relaxed muscles and search for support, an expression of
impotence. My mind registered this, but my self-respect was
utterly numbed, and I did not care.

I do not know how Hilda spent the day. I did not see her
again. She lunched upstairs with Michael, and towards evening I recovered enough self-command to get myself out of the
house and away to the station. No thought of renewing the
struggle crossed my mind. I knew now that the thing would
happen as surely as if it had been ordained from the beginning

of time. A queer fatalism came upon me. It seemed the fitting culmination of all that I had endured during the past years, the inevitable end which I ought to have foreknown.

I suppose that my state of mind was the result of psychological exhaustion. I have thought since that if I had stayed and tried again, fought to the last moment—but no, I know it would have been useless. And it is better that I should know it.

So I went away to Town, leaving Marling to Hilda and her chosen husband. I left word with Mrs. Marshall that they were to stay as long as they wished. I did not think that they would stay very long now, unless Michael were actually too ill to be moved.

X V

S O FAR AS MY RECORD CONCERNS MICHAEL BRISTOWE PER-
sonally, it is over. And if I were writing that report which
Hilda, still counting the cost over there in London, no doubt
thinks I am writing, I should have stopped already, for I never saw
him again after that strange evening in the library at Marling.
His performance that evening was, as Hilda said, nothing but a
flash, and, so far as I am aware, the last flash of that enigmatical
life. He lived, of course, for some time afterwards, and when,
married to Hilda and supported by her, he found refuge in the
sunny little cottage on the South Downs above the sea, he even
for a time recovered some measure of physical health. But the
delicate spring of his vitality was broken; there were no more
adventures for him, no more possibility of adventure, and the
next slight carelessness when the cold weather came again
(Hilda could not always be there—she was the bread-winner),
brought his old enemy again upon him. I do not imagine he
put up much of a resistance.

I saw the news of his death in the paper, and found myself
wincing at the mere name, as if the months had done nothing
to restore me to tranquillity. Yet, by this time, I was, in a sense,
living a normal life again.

I cannot write much of those intervening months, nor is it
necessary. They were an eternity for me, but a monotonous
eternity. I had stayed on in London helplessly, unable to go

any nearer to Hilda and her unholy experiment, and unable to drag myself farther away. I ought, of course, to have gone at once to the other side of the world, as I am going now, but I needed occasion to come and take me by the scruff of the neck, as, in the person of Lady Beryl Summers, it has now taken me. But, perhaps, even so, it would have been useless then. One is animal-like in these matters, and must linger for a time around the empty rat-hole, excited nerves still stronger than disillusioned brain.

I had been afraid that Hilda would try to insist on my presence at her wedding, especially as a note I had received from her a few days after I left Marling showed that she did not, even yet, realise the force of the blow that she had dealt me. But she did not make this impossible request. She wrote to me afterwards from the downland cottage—a brisk practical letter, giving merely formal particulars. To know the fact actually accomplished was merely like an acuter throb in the dull aching of a septic tooth, in my solitary, mooning existence.

I had let everyone suppose that I was still in the country for some time after my return, and had led the life of a recluse. Accident and my sister pulled me out of this morbid mode of existence after a time, and gradually I returned to some lifeless imitation of my old life. There are supports and safeguards in this civilised life of ours—habits, obligations, promptings. I do not wonder that in more primitive conditions men under similar stresses often deteriorate utterly. The mere presence of servants is a help against abjectness. I drank myself stupid one night when the thought of Hilda was unbearable, but the look in my man's eyes prevented me from doing it a second time.

And so the months passed by and many things happened, international events, political events, literary events, social events. I visited and was visited, entertained, and was invited again. I even wrote a little at times, though not well. And yet it seemed that life stood still and stagnant, so that the first event after Hilda's marriage seemed to be when Michael's name in the papers arrested me with that distressing jar. And when I laughed painfully a moment later, as I read the paragraph that followed describing how Mr. Bristowe had at one time been well known for his unusual gifts as a *clairvoyant* and had greatly assisted the police in clearing up a famous murder mystery, it seemed, bitter as it was, to be the first laugh that had passed my lips since I had parted with Hilda in the garden at Marling.

Yet the little stir passed quickly and left me unmoved again. The news could mean nothing to me in actual fact. I no longer felt any interest in Michael's potentialities, nor cared that they should be lost to the world for ever. I wondered apathetically what marks the last months might have left on Hilda, but it did not seem to matter. She no longer seemed now to be the girl that I had loved: that girl seemed to have died the day that she had embarked on her inadmissible enterprise. Her continued physical existence was merely an intolerable paradox, on which, for my sanity's sake, I had learnt not to dwell.

I did not write when I saw the news. It did not appear to be necessary. Our correspondence of brisk informative letters on her side and brief notes on mine had dwindled and dropped long ago. I had heard nothing of them from any source for many weeks.

Then, about a fortnight after I had seen the notice, she wrote and asked me to go down and see her, saying frankly that she needed my advice and help. My first impulse was to put the letter on the fire, so fiercely did I resent this careless attempt to reopen my wound. But there was a phrase near the end of the letter that caught at me in spite of myself. It might have been written lightly, half chaffingly, but I suspected that it was not. "You are the nearest thing to a brother that I possess." Even considered as chaff, there seemed to be a pathos in the words, coming from the self-reliant Hilda.

So I went. I could not, after all, endure to think of her alone and in difficulties, whatever the pain of the meeting to me. But I went with deliberate effort, not as the moth back to the candle. I knew too well—no man as introspective as I am can deceive himself in such matters—that what I had loved was in the past. It could not exist now. But I was going to be horribly reminded of it.

Yet it had been, after all, so short a time since we had parted in the garden at Marling. When I thought back to it, the mood and the atmosphere of that time came back so vividly that I could almost imagine that I was still living in those days of hope and uneasiness. For a moment the gulf made by the complete overturn of sentiments, hopes and life-plans was bridged, and present realities, when they came back, would come back with a jar. It is curious how the phase of one's life in which one has been most interested, has lived most intensely, may still dominate one's imagination sometimes for years afterwards. It remains in some way the norm, the criterion, of subsequent experience. No doubt, psychologists will some day measure the duration of such influences. One changes one's body entirely in the space of seven years, it is said; perhaps, one's brain and one's mind change with it, so that, until time has made distinct progress with the work of transforming one into another person, the effect of strong experience cannot begin to disappear.

And, after all, my meeting with Hilda was oddly hushed. I think that in every meeting emotionally anticipated, there must be something of anticlimax. The personality which has come to loom so large in imagination appears in the form of a small, concrete, human frame, moving and talking, in the human manner, like an animated puppet. The queer flatness of human intercourse, like the notes of a harpsichord, impresses one at such moments of reunion. Then, too, Hilda, as might have been expected, had lost vitality. She spoke quietly and a little draggingly, as though she were very tired. Even her shining hair had lost something of its lustre. But she spoke straightly, and held herself erect as ever. There was no such terrible change as I had half expected.

Nothing could have been less like our last tempestuous conversation. It was like the calm morning after the storm, when, with a queer sense of leisure and emptiness, one looks about to see what the damage has been. The furniture of Hilda's Bloomsbury flat distributed about the light little cottage living-room seemed like jetsam rescued from the sea, and the little servant like a shipwrecked mariner. The unreality of an excessive commonplaceness gripped us.

After the first conventional greetings—and we were punctiliously conventional—Hilda surprised me by putting into words my own thought of herself:

"You are looking very tired, Ralph!"

I said that there was nothing wrong with me, and asked her to tell me at once how I could be of assistance to her.

THE MAN WITH SIX SENSES

She told me gravely without any trace of self-consciousness. It was a pitiful little difficulty, which wrung my heart by its sheer pettiness—simply a phase of the money trouble which I had foreseen. The illness which had preceded Michael's death had used up all their reserves. An instalment of his tiny income was now due which, if she could get it, would be enough to help her over the crisis; but he had died intestate, and there was some delay and difficulty. The doctor would not let her go in and out of Town to see to the necessary formalities.

"The doctor!" I glanced at her in alarm. And then I understood. It was not yet certain that her sacrifice had been for nothing—nor was Michael Bristowe yet completely finished with. I hurried on before she could speak, asking questions about the business problem. I suggested that I could easily advance the money, and should be glad to do so, but she did not seem to wish that.

"It only needs someone to interview the solicitor," she assured me. "I would go myself—but I daren't take any risks. Almost everything is paid… Mrs. Hastings has got a temporary substitute; but, of course, she can't go on paying me as well in the meantime. It has made things rather difficult… But if I can get this, I can carry on all right." A change in her expression at the mere idea of the relief told me that the pressure was greater than she had let me know—perhaps a landlord dunning for rent, perhaps provision for immediate necessities lacking.

And it was twenty pounds! I wanted to weep for the sheer pity and irony of it. I would gladly have paid ten times as much to be spared the wrench to my feelings. But, obviously, the most helpful thing I could do was to promise that I would see the solicitor and do my best.

I added tentatively, "Your aunt? Is there any chance of her coming over soon?"

Hilda shook her head and answered my intention: "No, I can't bring her over. She can't stand English winters now... But there is an old friend of mine who helps to run a nursing-home. I am going to her later on."

I questioned her a little further as tactfully as I could. It was distressing to me to do so, the more that I felt a certain painful ludicrousness in my position; but I suspected that there was no one else who would even ask a question.

I found, as I might have expected, that her arrangements were admirable. Michael's child was to have every chance. I divined, as we talked, though she was reticent, that Michael's child was now the centre of all her hopes and ambitions. It must, in fact, be her sole remaining hope. That was why, even after all that she must have gone through, she showed no sign of demoralisation. She was keeping going and keeping her poise for this reason. But I felt that there was more effort in it than there had ever been before. It had become conscious. It had to be maintained against strain.

I wondered more than ever about Michael Bristowe, and how he had conducted himself during those last months of his life. But about that I asked no questions. Her obvious fatigue was my best evidence. She told me very little about it, then or at any time, and what I learnt I gathered from allusions. For her, it must have been a life of sickening strain with no compensating touch of dignity. At times in his career, Michael Bristowe had been impressive, though always difficult and dangerous to deal with. But there was no ennobling element of dangerousness in the fretful neurasthenic that she had married. I had been sure in the old days that she had sometimes been afraid that Michael, in one of his desperate moods, might commit suicide, though the word was never mentioned between us. But the Michael Bristowe of these last days had no longer the spirit to make even a suicide. He just became more and more of a crank. There were more and more things that he could not endure. He had to be kept in an isolation that became constantly more complete, while Hilda tried to fulfil the function of vacuum chamber between him and the world. And so on, with life becoming more and more impossible, until, mercifully, he got the chill that finished him. Certainly, he went in no blaze of glory, this Messiah, not even the dark glory of a crucifixion. One can only express it in the indignity of modern slang. He fizzled out. I suppose that this is the most that we can expect of our Messiahs in this Age of Lead.

I left Hilda as soon as I reasonably could. My very spirit was sick within me. And, apart from my own feelings, I could not be sure, grotesque as the supposition seemed, that I might not strain her resources if I stayed to lunch. Nevertheless, I thought that she clung to my company a little when I came to say good-bye. Yet there was so little that I could do. She had to face alone a dreary, yet hazardous, period of waiting. I wondered, what I could never ask, whether she still thought that her experiment had been worth while. Perhaps she did, with Michael's child to hope for. It seemed to me that she had stilled her spirit, driven fears and misgivings under by sheer force of will, in order to make smooth the path for this young prince to come into his kingdom.

XVI

HILDA'S CHILD WAS BORN IN HER FRIEND'S NURSING-home early in the spring of the New Year. It was a girl. Hilda was very ill, a long dragging illness, not dangerous after the first fortnight, but a tedious weakness and disability—such an illness as she had not calculated upon, never before having had reason to distrust her magnificent health. But I suppose that nervous strain cannot always be discounted by will-power.

I was able to see her for the first time one April day when the sun was shining and the air exhilarating even in London, as it had been the day a year before when she had come to me in the garden at Marling and had predicted, or rather, one might almost say, had planned, all that had subsequently happened to her. She was in an invalid chair by the open window of a large light room looking out over a quiet West-End square of turf and budding trees. Her friend, Lettice Platt, had seen to it that she had the most favourable conditions possible. Miss Platt was a plump, plain, young woman with honest and intelligent eyes, and of the type obviously born to mother other people's children. It had been almost with a groan of relief that I had seen Hilda safe into her competent keeping.

Hilda, lying back in her chair, had a look of fragility that made her strange to me. Her cheeks were pale and her manner listless. But she was evidently pleased to see me, and ready to attend to the business information that I had for her. Her illness had, of course, thrown out anew her financial calculations, and it had been necessary for me, in response to a message from her, to arrange with her own solicitors for an advance to meet the emergency. Her face cleared, as I explained that the difficulty had been overcome.

"Lettice has been paying for me to stay on here out of her own pocket," she explained, a slight flush disturbing her pallor; "I couldn't have let it go on much longer."

"You are lucky to have a friend like Miss Platt," I remarked casually.

"I am lucky in having more than one friend who sticks to me."

I knew that the tears standing in her eyes, and the quiver of sentiment in her voice, were only signs of physical weakness, but they were so unlike Hilda's usual, clean-cut, controlled manner that I found myself embarrassed. I was glad that Miss Platt, entering the room with the child at the moment, made it unnecessary for me to make any reply.

I had seen Hilda's daughter before, when I had called to enquire at the Home. By all the rules of the game, I ought to have hated the sight of the little creature with Michael's dark eyes and hair. But this affair had been outside the rules of the game from the beginning. I found that I could not hate little Stella. She was too small and helpless. The high destiny for which she had been born (apart from which she never would have been born at all) seemed pathetic when one looked at the minute fumbling fingers which might or might not have in them the new magic sensibility. No one could tell yet. At present no one could be certain that she was not blind, or deaf, or idiot. The weight resting on her tiny personality seemed too heavy.

To me, it seems a hard fate for any child to be born dedicate; and I cannot help suspecting that it may be the happiest thing for little Stella if she turns out, after all, to be completely commonplace.

Miss Platt had told me already of Hilda's disappointment that the baby had not been a boy, and something in Hilda's attitude as she reached and took her reminded me again that she had always thought and spoken of the coming child as a son. That was one thing that had not gone according to plan. Master of Arts as she was, and as much of a feminist as are most educated women nowadays, Hilda, like any Victorian, had attached her exceptional hopes to a young prince. Involuntarily, it flashed across my mind, as she took the child from Miss Platt, that perhaps a woman finds difficulty in seeing herself as Madonna towards an infant of her own sex. I was distressed and ashamed of the thought the next moment. And yet, the very fact that I could even hint to myself such a conjecture about Hilda—I suspect now that this was in truth the first painful step to my painful recovery.

I do not quite know how the suggestion reached me from Hilda's manner at this moment. She handled the child gently, and looked at her quietly, as she lay in her arms, and smiled when I praised her. Perhaps, it was all a shade too quiet for an enthusiastic young mother; but then, after all, she was still obviously very weak. And it might have been merely in consideration for me that she changed the subject almost at once, and asked me about outside events, and listened while I gave her a flow of social gossip such as she had never shown much interest in of old, but now seemed to swallow with the avidity of isolation.

When tea was brought, she seized the opportunity to give the baby back to the nurse, and this time my impression was more definite.

"Here, take her, nurse. She's getting too heavy for me."

It was the first time that I had ever heard fretfulness in Hilda's voice, and I felt that I wanted to turn away my eyes. But I went on talking as if I had noticed nothing unexpected, and she regained her equanimity immediately.

As I was leaving, I stopped to speak to Miss Platt in an outer room. What I had observed had puzzled and worried me, and I wanted, if possible, to gather a little more information. She and I had become good friends in the last weeks, and had discussed Hilda's case together, though with reticence, since I did not know how far she was in Hilda's confidence, or whether she understood what had been the truth behind her marriage to Michael Bristowe. I enquired casually now whether Hilda had the child with her very much.

Miss Platt's very shrewd eyes regarded me with a comprehending smile. "Ah! You've noticed... And now, of course, you're upset, like most men, when they find that all women haven't the maternal instincts of a broody hen... Don't worry, Mr. Standring. Young mothers quite frequently show a slight aversion for their offspring just at first. After all, they've had so much trouble about it, you see, and the result really does look so inadequate. It will be all right, later on. When the kiddy begins to smile back, and make sounds and that sort of thing, the mother begins to take an interest again. Affection without any response at all isn't really very common, even in mothers... You'll see. It will be all right."

I had got used to Miss Platt's free tongue, and I bowed to her sagacity and experience, and hoped that it would be all as she said. But it was evident to me now that she had no knowledge of the peculiar circumstances of Hilda's case.

And that, too, in itself, was a minor puzzle. Why had Hilda, the soul of frankness, not told her friend the truth about her marriage to Michael Bristowe? I knew that they had not met for some time previously to Hilda's recent emergency; but, in these weeks of her illness, there must have been opportunity enough. If Hilda's attitude towards what she had done had remained precisely what it had been when she had discussed the subject so freely and fully with me at Marling, it was inconceivable that she should not have confided the whole matter to her friend and helper. Yet she had not done so.

I came back to the still unsolved puzzle of her attitude to the baby Stella. It was impossible to think of the old rational Hilda caring the less about the child because of the, after all, irrelevant fact that she was not a boy. Poor little Stella! As I glanced at her again, lying asleep in her cot, unloved even by the mother who had brought her into the world with such serious and strenuous purpose, I felt a pang of sympathy. It was as if the sleeping infant and I were fellow victims.

I did not pursue any further my conversation with Miss Platt. It came to me suddenly that I did not want to know the answer to the problem. At the same time, with a surge of irritation and impatience that I could not control, I realised that I should probably be compelled to watch that answer evolve itself.

XVII

I AM NEARLY AT THE END. IT WAS ONLY A WEEK OR TWO after that visit to the nursing-home that I received Lady Beryl's offer, and jumped at it with an eagerness that surprised myself. I had become unofficially Hilda's man of business during this time; rather more than that, her chief link with the outside world. She has friends enough, but not, I imagine, many intimate ones. I doubt if anyone besides myself knows the complete story of the last two years. I know that her devotion to Michael even before her marriage had somewhat isolated her from her old circle of comrades of school and university days. One so soon drops out in London. Anyhow, whatever the explanation, and although we talked very little of the more recent past but far more of the more distant times of our childhood and schooldays, she was obviously becoming more and more dependent upon my society.

In this matter, I had little choice; circumstances yet again made me their puppet. I could not desert her in her necessity, though I think she innocently demanded more of me than ought to be demanded of any man. I have been to her during these months the brother that she called me in that letter that renewed our relations, and have done violence to myself in the process. It is not that I am still in love with her. Prolonged suffering of the kind that she put me through becomes eventually its own anæsthetic. The capacity is destroyed, like lung tissue in phthisis, so that one will never feel, or breathe, so fully again. And thus one recovers, as I know now that I shall recover. My life is not shattered. It might be comforting if I could suppose that it were. But I am not now a young man, and I know that these things come to an end. It adds another sting to the grief of maturity that one knows that the grief itself will not be lasting. Hilda and I may come together again some day and be happy. We shall not be the same people who have lived and suffered in these last years. Their suffering is beyond remedy.

In the meantime, the conviction grew upon me that I must get away from her. Such a medley of emotions is more than one can be expected to endure for any length of time. One must release oneself. I realise now that the passion to get clear away had been rising in me for months. And then mercifully, most opportunely, just when Hilda's returning health made it possible for me to go without brutality, came Lady Beryl's offer. Two years ago I should have laughed if anyone had told me that I was to become the chronicler of the deeds of an exploring expedition searching for the lost race of Incas in the hinterland of Peru. The wanderlust is a new experience for me. Yet so it is. I happened—it was only a month ago, though it seems far longer—lightly to mention my restlessness in the impulsive lady's presence. After that, nothing would do but that I should go: a "highbrow" writer to describe the adventures of the expedition "in real literary style," in addition to the commonplace newspaper correspondent, became immediately a *sine qua non* of her project.

Hilda was sufficiently herself again to take the news of my decision very quietly, though instinct told me that it was something of a shock to her. She asked one or two questions, and gave no hint of any kind of opposition to the idea; on the other hand, she gave me none of the eager encouragement which any such enterprise would certainly have brought from her in the old days.

She had little Stella out in her perambulator in the Square gardens on the sunny June morning when I called to say good-bye, and I went across to join her. I was selfishly glad that I should still be leaving her in the care of the competent Miss Platt, though she was to leave the Home in the following week. It seemed to lessen my own responsibility. She expected to be back at work again in a few weeks' time, a highly trained nurse for Stella having already been engaged. On the material side, Hilda's affairs were straightening themselves out, and I could go without misgiving.

And yet, as I saw her sitting beside the pram in that little green oasis of the big city, doing nothing, and gazing, not at her baby, but into the distance with an expression which I could not interpret, I felt an utterly unreasonable sense of guilt. The face which she turned to me had recovered its fine grave beauty, but there was something gone. And it was the some-thing whose presence or absence is almost more important for the individual's struggle with life than the most favourable or malign of circumstances—her confidence. And yet she made so brave a show to hide the lack, that no one with less knowledge of her than I possessed would have guessed. I suppose that the strongest of us has his vulnerable spot. Long, slow illness seems to have found Hilda's. I do not think that anything else could have daunted her. Perhaps, with regained health, she will be able to build again on a firmer basis. God knows, I hope so. She cannot be again the girl that I loved, but I suppose, as I try to look at it disinterestedly, that she may yet be as noble a woman as she was a girl.

It was an occasion when the conversation had to be superficial and of trivialities. We talked of the voyage, of my equipment, and the plans of the expedition; very little of her plans, very little of the child that was lying asleep beside us. It is difficult to forgive myself when I think now of Hilda's face and remember that there was a quite unquenchable surge of triumph in me as we talked. This time it was I that was going away, adventuring, to new countries and new experience, while she was staying to a humdrum existence of routine work, of waiting and thinking and, perhaps, regretting. I had never realised that there had been in my wretchedness of the last year this element also—this shame that I was relegated to the feminine rôle of waiting and watching, while Hilda dared. I should have dismissed it as monstrous that any such sentiment could have a part in my thoughts, if this sudden exultation of my recovered manhood had not risen to witness against me.

Although I was careful, perhaps Hilda felt something of what I was trying to conceal. And perhaps that was why she chose this moment to ask me to make my record of what I knew of Michael Bristowe. She had to hold on to what she had. The next moment brought me fresh evidence of what was in her mind.

Little Stella suddenly asserted herself. She wakened and began to whimper and to move her little hands under her shawl.

Hilda's eyes brightened suddenly, as she looked at her baby.

"Do you see?" she said in an almost awe-stricken whisper, "she's trying to get her hands free."

I assented, though the allusion jarred me. I had not the heart to point out, what she might surely have known as well as I, that one rarely sees a small wrapped-up baby that is not trying to get its hands free. It was the first revelation to me how intensely, how desperately, Hilda was clinging to the hope that her sacrifice had not been in vain.

The knowledge shook me. We were walking back to the Home now, and moved on in silence for a few seconds. I noticed nursemaids and the few scattered morning pedestrians of a London square glancing at us with a mixture of approval and amusement. We must have looked like a devoted young couple giving our common offspring an airing. I wondered in that relaxed moment if, after all, I had not better make their idea as nearly true as it was now possible to make it. I thought it probable that, if I proposed to her now, Hilda would accept me. She was fond of me, and grateful to me, and she needed the security that I could give. She did not want me to go away.

It was only a momentary flight of fancy. I knew that I should not do it because I did not really want to. It would be too gross a treachery to my old dreams to marry Hilda after this fashion. It would outrage my inner self in a way that I should have to pay for too heavily—that we should both have to pay for. The idea of marrying a widow has always been distasteful to me. That the widow was Hilda seemed to make it unthinkable. Whether the Hilda I loved ever really existed or not, it is certain that she no longer exists now. I could not set in her place this jaded, yet still gallant, woman, with whom, nevertheless, I feel I have still a tie and even a reluctant tender sympathy.

If Hilda had loved me, that might have forced my hand. But she did not love me, though she was beginning to turn to

me. As we said good-bye, after all, at the corner of the square,
though we were brisk and cheerful, the tears stood in her eyes.
But I understand too well that it is a change of mental attitude
rather than the rise of a spontaneous emotion. Her suffering has
taught her that life is, and must be, chiefly ruled by Fear—that
the man who tries to practise ideals in this world is like one
who composes an Ode to Peace while the enemy is setting fire
to the thatch. The world is no longer her oyster—the oyster of
her intellect. She begins to understand, too, in what elementary
manner one needs the help and support of one's fellow creatures, the comfort of contact. She begins to realise, perhaps,
those profound needs and emotions which rise in the integrity
of the organism itself, and that it is not shortsightedness nor
selfishness to give these preference over everything else, but a
mere condition of existence.

Yet I feel little exultation in the incipient fulfilment of my
prophecies. After all, the young Hilda of eighteen months ago
made a valiant attempt, out of the common rut. She found a
novel situation, and, as she could, she rose to it. It would be a
poor thing to triumph over one who has made an effort beyond
human strength because, when the thing was accomplished,
her strength failed and she fell below herself in compensation.
After all, little Stella is there. She may have her father's strange
capacity—the more, perhaps (to go by the little we know of
the laws of heredity), that she is a princess, and not a prince.
She may grow to strange heights of understanding, and, even
as Hilda planned, begin a new era of knowledge and power for
mankind. Hilda may have no emotional fondness for her, but
she will not fail her in any other way. No child will have better
care or finer training. The result is on the knees of the gods.

When I come back, if I come back at all (for our expedition will not be without its perils), it may be possible to see farther into the future.

And if the experiment represented by Stella's existence succeeds, will it have been worth while? Was Hilda right? Is all that she has suffered and all that I have suffered—is what I can still only feel to be an outrage on Nature, justified? Is there a meaning in all this, or is it merely another piece of vulgar nonsense scribbled by the divine hobbledehoy upon the wall of Time? I know no more than when I started. I have not solved the problem, but I have satisfied myself that it is insoluble. I can put it behind me.

In a few days now we reach Lima. Already, we have passed the great Canal, and I have felt a new world about me. It is interesting. It interests me more than I should have thought possible. I have never felt the lure of geographical adventure before. I have laughed at others who felt it. Now, I feel that I owe them an apology.

The proportions of all that I have left seem to be shrinking, and I look forward eagerly to our fresh life of day-to-day living, with only a vague goal before us and a sharp spice of danger to give full flavour to our adventure. I am sure that we modern men plot and plan too much, look too far ahead, take our responsibility too heavily. The old *conquistadors* who came first to these regions from our world were not like that. Humbly, a small boy again, I take them as my model:

"To-morrow to fresh woods and pastures new."

AFTERWORD

Muriel Jaeger's Educated Woman and the New Nativity Narrative

This essay first appeared as chapter five of Dangerous by
Degrees: Women at Oxford and the Somerville College
Novelists *by Susan J. Leonardi, published by Rutgers University
Press in 1989. The book explored the work of several novelists
who, like Jaeger, studied at Somerville College and were among
the first women to receive a degree from Oxford University. These
pioneering authors include Vera Brittain, Winifred Holtby,
Dorothy L. Sayers, Doreen Wallace and Margaret Kennedy.*

Muriel Jaeger, the "Jim" of Sayers' early letters and member
of the Mutual Admiration Society, is the least known and the
least prolific of these Somerville novelists. Though she wrote
a play and three short novels, most of her work is nonfiction
and little of it directly addresses the topic of the educated
woman or women's role in the world. Like Sayers, however,
she takes for granted a woman's right to whatever life she
chooses. In her chapter on George Sand in *Experimental Lives*,
a collection of biographical pieces, she praises the courage
and conviction of the woman who chooses to break new
ground. "People—especially women—have certainly been
freer because one immensely courageous and highly vocal

woman explored the uncleared country for them." A book of essays published late in Jaeger's life, *Shepherd's Trade*, complains good-humouredly about the hazards of being such a "vocal woman." She and her writing friends have suffered, she says, from the story of Jane Austen writing "her books with easy placidity in the common sitting-room, putting them aside at every domestic and social demand and calmly resuming them when the interruption was over." Jaeger suggests that the story is not truth but fiction, used to chide women writers who express the "difficulties of authorship in our harassed existences."

Her fiction, with the exception of *The Man with Six Senses*, addresses these issues only obliquely. In the earliest novel, an ironic utopian fiction called *The Question Mark*, the protagonists are all male, and her portrait of the twenty-second century is unremittingly man-centred. She does, in good utopian fashion, describe the relationship between the men and women in her future society: in the "normal" class, the future looks worse for women than the present. Ena, a "normal" woman, tells Guy, the twentieth-century man transplanted into the twenty-second century, "You're not like the rest. You don't think girls are for nothing but to tease and make love to." More alarming than this implied limitation of women's role, there has developed in this new society a fashion for harems. Yet in the "intellectual" class, women are theoretically equal; this suggests that education not only determines class but levels sex. But like the division of future humans in *The Time Machine* this division into "normal" and "intellectual" has robbed each class of important human qualities. Sylvia, the "intellectual" woman in the novel, has an exciting and independent life, but both she and her fiancé are

rather detached, cold sorts, having, apparently, sacrificed heart
for head.

Sylvia plays a minor role in *The Question Mark*, but in Jaeger's
next novel, *The Man with Six Senses*, the figure of the educated
woman, though she is neither the eponymous subject nor
the narrator of this quirky book, is the centre of all energy
and activity. An Oxbridge graduate, a confident, independent, career-minded woman, Hilda takes on the "man with
six senses," Michael Bristowe, and with him the future of
humankind. However, before we examine this portrayal of the
educated woman and her unusual adventure, we must look at
the portrayal of the narrator through whose eyes we see her,
lest, unwary readers, we be seduced by his sophistication and
disarming common sense into reading only *his* version of the
story.

An intelligent, patronising, and pedantic man, the narrator, Ralph, mirrors closely those Oxford males who, quite
supportive of degrees for women, saw the educated woman
primarily as a complement to the educated man. Himself a
"highly educated man," an intellectual, a writer of essays,
Ralph wants to marry the beautiful Hilda. Both their families
have plotted the union, but both sets of parents are dead by
the time Hilda finishes her university degree. Ralph, several
years older than she, has watched her grow up and has become
convinced that she is exactly suited to him. His mother, while
she was still alive, wanted him to propose to the eighteen-
year-old Hilda, but Ralph decided to wait because, unlike his
mother, he quite approves of his future wife's educational
aspirations. His mother, he says, "did not understand nor
accept our later maturing, due to the increasingly complicated

demands of civilised and cultured life, which make a longer
period of growth essential if a completely adequate personality is to emerge."

Ralph congratulates himself on his liberal attitude—"I have
never been against the higher education of women, as, openly
or covertly, are many of my contemporaries"—but immediately
follows this declaration with a shift of focus that reveals what
is to him the chief benefit of this higher education: "I think an
educated man all the better for having an educated wife, who
is able to be an intellectual companion to him, to be interested in his work, and to follow the movements of his mind."
Though few of his contemporaries would have approved so
enthusiastically of a university education, not just for women
in general, but for their intended wives, Ralph's diction nevertheless constantly betrays his failure to see Hilda as a human
being. He imagines her, for example, "as the young heroine
of an old Teutonic epic or of an Icelandic saga." Later, when
she is staying at Marling, Ralph's home, he sees her "as the
Princess of Thule... bestowing gifts in her father's high hall."
Thus while he casts her as a heroine, almost a goddess, equally
he relishes having her under his roof and rule. That his home
becomes "her father's high hall" indicates the paternal attitude
which he assumes is constitutive of marriage and in which he
frequently indulges. While on the one hand he idealises Hilda
as more-than-human, on the other he frequently characterises
her as less than himself and dependent upon him: "Young and
innocent," "unawakened," attractively shy and immature, "a
lonely and pathetic figure in need of my help and protection,"
"a child still—the precious child whom I loved and had to save,
at all costs, from herself."

When Hilda does not live up or down to his expectations, he is disappointed. When she comes back from college, for example, a "self-possessed girl who welcomed me so graciously in the pleasantly austere sitting-room," who had "just that additional confidence, that social aplomb, which I had counted on her gaining," he "missed the old shyness." Not only does she disconcert him with her newly acquired social confidence, but she also destroys his vision of himself as "welcome rescuer" and admired mentor. Instead of the enthusiastic praise for his book and a pupil's interest in its subject matter, she discusses his theses as an equal. "I suppose," he comments, "that one is liable to forget as one grows older the possibilities of rapid mental development in the early twenties." Even, then, when she demonstrates her ability to be an intellectual companion, he notes condescendingly, as one would of a child, how much she has grown. And he admits that this new Hilda was "not entirely welcome to a man coming in search of solace."

Ralph's need for solace is occasioned by an affair he had in Italy which, he implies, turned out rather badly. Though he allows himself the licence of other relationships, even sexual ones, he is jealous and resentful of Hilda's nonsexual interest in Michael Bristowe. And though Ralph himself is absorbed in his work, he is sure that Hilda does not take hers very seriously and resents her refusal of his marriage proposal on grounds that she likes what she is doing. He does not suggest that she could continue working after marriage, because a wife should interest herself in *his* work and "follow the movements of his mind." While both his sexual experience and his devotion to work seem natural to him, he can accept neither in Hilda. Later in the novel, after her husband's death, Ralph decides not to

renew his proposal of marriage, because "the idea of marrying a widow has always been distasteful to me." He does not
explain his distaste, but one assumes that it is rooted in the kind
of possessiveness Doreen Wallace's Margery in *The Time of Wild
Roses* describes so cynically: "If there is one thing which will
turn a man from a rational human being into a he-ape incapable of thought, it is the notion that another male is sharing
the body of his female." Though the other male in this case is
dead and was never anyone Hilda desired sexually, Ralph does
not even attempt to explore, much less overcome, the irrational
"distaste." It is there; it seems altogether natural to him. Indeed
the romance plot depends on woman-as-virgin-waiting-to-be-
awakened. Thus Ralph not only writes out but judges his own
experience in terms of this plot.

What Ralph ultimately resents most about Hilda is her
rationality. A traditional complaint of men about women is
that they are irrational. Yet it is this very irrationality which
gives men power over women and easy grounds for dismissing
their claims. While Ralph sees rationality as highly desirable in
a helpmate, while the acquisition of rationality strikes him as
a good effect of the education of women, its actual presence
in Hilda disconcerts and angers him because it diminishes his
power and augments her claims. By being rational, Hilda devi-
ates from both roles he has cast her in: she is neither mythi-
cal nor helpless. Besides her failure to live up to his fantasies,
this rational woman argues with his work, as we have seen,
and points out his specious arguments. Furthermore, as if
rationality leaves no room for romantic myths, her rational
approach to life seems to make her immune to falling in love.
Ralph expects at least a spark of ardour from his proposal of

marriage, but Hilda only answers calmly, "It's pleasant to know that you want me, Ralph," as she refuses him. He expects to dissuade her from what he regards as her destructive plan for life. When she says she has tried to be as rational and practical as she can, he attacks her: "Rational! It's rationality that is the matter with you." Ralph wants Hilda to be irrational so he can use that irrationality to manipulate her: "I felt sometimes that if I could only get Hilda to waver in her poise for a moment, to say something thoroughly irrational and unjust, to lose her temper, there might have been a chance to make progress," progress meaning, to Ralph, the possession of Hilda.

Ralph's most significant and self-revelatory attack on Hilda's rationality is his admission that, having lost a simple argument in which he was using an irrational generalisation about women to convince her to give up her work, "I went away in impotent rage against the rational woman and all her works." The choice of words here, like the rhetoric of male Oxford, reveals the intense emotions conjured up by the figure of the woman with a degree. First, the use of "impotent" suggests fear that educated woman emasculates: not only is Ralph unable to find a hole in her reasoning, not only, that is, is he intellectually defeated by this young woman, but in his eyes her refusal to marry him threatens and/or effects impotence as well. While he looks to the educated woman as fit helpmate, she quickly becomes his equal and insists on such independent action as turning down his proposal of marriage, thus depriving him of those powerful symbols of potency, a wife and children.

Second, "rage" suggests that underneath his own rational veneer Ralph himself is irrational; in spite of his ostensible approval of the idea of educated women, the actuality threatens to strip him of the fruits of his own education. That civilised, cultivated life of the mind, nurtured by the university, so long a prerogative of men, rests perhaps, like male power itself, on displacing its opposite onto the other sex. When that is no longer possible, when women claim a right to such an educated life, men experience the irrationality in themselves, here as rage. Finally, the reference here to the baptismal formula in which the person to be christened is asked to denounce Satan and all his works, suggests the extreme response, so far from Ralph's conscious thought, to education for women—that it is diabolical, that it turns women from angels to devils, from willing servants to adamant rebels against the rule of the male god. It was, further, a woman's lust for the fruit of the tree of knowledge which allied her to Satan in the first place, according to Christian myth. Ralph's rhetoric implies this connection between the Eve wanting to be educated and the educated Hilda, and simultaneously asserts his own position on the side of the angels. That both men in the text have angels' names (Raphael, Michael) underscores this gendered alignment and hints, perhaps, at a covert alliance between the men. In any case, Ralph's apparent feminist sympathies work only at the level of his rhetoric and function only when they result in his own aggrandisement. He relishes the vision of himself as tolerant and forward-looking in his approval of women's education and independence but is unable and unwilling to accept the consequences of this attitude.

Besides lashing out in rage, he resorts to the most traditional clichés about women and thus suggests that the educated woman is not at all what he really wants for himself. When Hilda announces her plan to marry Michael Bristowe, an arrangement she regards as both practical and rational, Ralph cannot believe that "an adult woman should speak to me in this manner about the supreme experience of her sex." Ironically, in his desire for the child bride Hilda will never be, Ralph immediately decides Hilda is not, in fact, an adult woman. What he wants is a woman who does regard marriage as the supreme experience. That he adds "of her sex" indicates that marriage is not, of course, the supreme experience for his sex, for himself. He has, after all, his work; his wife should abandon hers and take up him as her job. The irrationality of this position can be ignored only by his positing a dichotomy between adult men and adult women. Unlike the adult man, who is independent, dedicated to his work, and able to see love and marriage in practical terms, a woman who acts and thinks likewise must be immature.

As Ralph has tried unsuccessfully to get Hilda to marry him, so he tries unsuccessfully to prevent her from marrying Michael Bristowe. In the conversation which follows Ralph's expression of "incredulity" about Hilda's willingness to marry without love, Hilda expounds her agnostic, evolutionary philosophy. Ralph comments that he "had had glimpses before of this philosophy of Hilda's." Again we see that Ralph, while approving of the educated woman in the abstract, has little interest in her in the concrete. He has not been interested enough to hear her expound her "philosophy," though he has repeatedly wanted to hear her accept his marriage proposal—that is, the content of her intellectual life is quite secondary to her sexual and social function as his future wife. That she is beautiful and intelligent is enough; only when she acts in a manner he finds incredible is he willing to listen to her exposition of the beliefs out of which she acts. Here, too, there is a suggestion of Ralph's irrationality. He has not heard Hilda because he has not been interested; he has not been interested because he has feared to hear, feared that Hilda is not the ideal woman he has set her up to be.

This carefully constructed contrast between Ralph's apparent approval of educated women, his tolerant, man-of-the-modern-world manner, and the fear and irrationality which underlies these attitudes, reveal him to be a partly unreliable narrator whose interpretation of Hilda and her story readers must constantly question. He admits at the outset, in fact, that his narrative is not "the account of Michael Bristowe's strange career that Hilda asked me to write." Requested to tell the story of another man and his special gift, Ralph, writer and egoist, can tell only the story which touches him more personally, the story of the educated woman and all her works. A woman's story, though, even an educated woman's story, is traditionally assumed to be a romance. Ralph therefore tells the story of a woman and a man, and in doing so he tells the story of himself because he assumes that Hilda, whom he regards as his "natural mate," can have no story apart from him. The text, however, though it presents the story only from Ralph's point of view, refuses to limit itself to his version. Hilda, in her attempt to alter the romantic script prescribed for her life, alters as well Ralph's narrative. Both Ralph's direct reports of conversations between him and Hilda and the ironies implicit in his self-portrait alert the reader to a subtext, a new story for the new woman—educated—whom the traditional romance plot cannot accommodate.

In order to sort out the elements of this new plot from the old, we must look briefly at the story Ralph tells. I present here the outline of that story, with little narrative comment, as a context from which to extract the threads of Hilda's more hidden narrative. As we have seen, Ralph has known Hilda for many years: he regards their marriage as "a long-standing family plot." When she leaves the university, she takes a job as secretary to "one of the political women who hoped to be in the next Parliament" and lives alone in a small Bloomsbury flat. Meanwhile Ralph has indulged his wish to travel and to become a man of the world. When he returns after some time in Italy, he finds Hilda equally desirable but changed not altogether to his liking. For one thing, she talks to him as an equal about his work. But the main problem is that she has taken up again the company of a man he regards as thoroughly undesirable, Michael Bristowe, who, Hilda has come to realise, has a strange and special gift. It manifests itself at first as a dowsing ability—that is, he can recognise the presence of water and other substances even underground. One day Hilda, Ralph, and Michael are out in the country; Michael, reacting violently to his sense of something horrible nearby, discovers a corpse. The journalist who subsequently tries to make use of Michael for police work writes of him as "a truly terrible young man" who "informed me... that the elderly gentleman of military appearance who shared our compartment... was wearing corsets with steel in them and that the pearls of the opulent-looking lady who had been sitting near us at luncheon were imitation. What a disturbing element Michael Bristowe would be to introduce into smart society!" Smart society, however, is little inclined to take up someone who detects not only metal and corpses but hypocrisy as well.

Hilda wants to help Michael because she thinks his gift significant, and she knows that he is an unreliable sort who has little ability to make his way in the world. After Michael fails as a detective and a finder of oil, jobless, he becomes extremely unhappy with himself, carelessly contracts pneumonia, and, Ralph says, would have died but for Hilda's determination that he recover. He does recover, in part, but is weak and constantly depressed, and when Hilda takes him to Marling, Ralph's house, to convalesce, Ralph begins to believe in the sixth sense, but he perceives it as alienating and menacing. An old dowser who recognises Michael's ability urges Hilda to look after Michael well because "There aren't many of his kind."

Because the dowser's injunction corresponds to her own sense of responsibility, Hilda decides to marry Michael. Michael is, she says, helpless without her, and she is convinced that "If *he* goes under, humanity may lose a chance that may never come again... And I'm the only person who can do anything." She does not love him; she only senses that he is her temporary responsibility. She knows, too, that he will die shortly and that "we may have a child..." to inherit his gift: "It's the only chance." Ralph is appalled at this turn of events. He is devastated by the death of his hopes of marrying his "natural mate" and incredulous that Hilda could be so unwomanly as to marry out of social responsibility rather than love. He has not been able to convince her to marry him, and nothing he says can change her mind about marrying Michael; when he accuses her of making Michael into a Messiah, she agrees, in so far as the "Michael Bristowes are the only sort of Messiahs we can expect now that we have lost our omnipotent God. Our God is one who needs our help. And it seems clear that this is my opportunity to help."

Ralph goes away for some months while Hilda and Michael marry and settle in the country. As Hilda and the doctors predicted, Michael does not live long. Ralph returns after Michael's death knowing that Hilda would no longer be the girl he loved: "that girl seemed to have died the day she embarked on her inadmissible enterprise." Ralph determines to stay away but Hilda writes to him urgently because she has no money and he is "the nearest thing to a brother that I possess." It is then that Ralph discovers that she is, indeed, pregnant with Michael's child. She has the baby in the nursing home of a friend, Lettice Platt; it is a hard delivery—both child and mother are ill afterwards. The surprising thing, what no one anticipated, is that "this young prince [coming] into his kingdom" turns out to be a girl. Hilda seems not terribly interested in the baby, which Ralph attributes to its sex and Lettice to Hilda's weakened state. But it is clear that Hilda remains hopeful that the child will have Michael's gift. Ralph accepts a journalism assignment on an expedition; she returns to her job. Ralph believes that Hilda would marry him at this point but, as we have seen, he is not interested in marrying a widow. He concludes his narrative with what he believes and desires that Hilda has learned from this experience,

> that life is, and must be, chiefly ruled by Fear—that the man who tries to practise ideals in this world is like one who composes an Ode to Peace while the enemy is setting fire to the Thatch. The world is no longer her oyster—the oyster of her intellect. She begins to understand too, in what elementary manner one needs the help and support of one's fellow creatures, the comfort of contact.

But he says he will not exult in the fulfilment of his prophesies, because Hilda did, after all, make a "valiant attempt":

"It would be a poor thing to triumph over one who has made an effort beyond human strength because, when the thing was accomplished, her strength failed and she fell below herself in compensation."

This is Ralph's version of the story and his patronising interpretation of its significance, an interpretation which projects his own values on the silent/silenced Hilda. In *Paradise Lost* Raphael tells Adam and Eve the story of the angels' rebellion and warns the pair that they, too, might fall. Similarly, Ralph sees in Hilda's failure to read/heed correctly the lesson of the old story—that is, to stop rebelling and to marry him—her fall, like Eve's a fall from innocence to experience, from trusting dependence to disillusioning independence. It is not surprising, then, that Ralph's antidote to this story is to insist even more adamantly on the romance plot: Hilda will either come to her senses and marry (admitting thereby her need for "the help and support of one's fellow creatures") or she will be punished by failing strength and/or death.

Clearly, Ralph's tendency to write the romance into Hilda's story, the resemblance of his rhetoric to that of male Oxford, and his oddly irrelevant and inflated rhetoric call his conclusions into question. Is Hilda now willing to marry Ralph? What has she really learned from her experience? What is its significance? And if Ralph's assessment is, indeed, accurate, what are we to make of the new, defeated Hilda? Since we have only Ralph's version of the story, which he confesses is not the story Hilda asked him to tell, we must look more closely at the story Hilda, in spite of Ralph, is trying to tell. First of all, Hilda has asked Ralph to write, not her story, but "the account of Michael Bristowe's strange career." Throughout the novel, Hilda has that objectivity, that "singleness of purpose that pursues knowledge" which Sayers attributes to the educated woman. Even her relationship to the man she marries is objective and purposeful: she is not in love with him, she simply feels a duty toward humanity. She realises, as well as Ralph does, how unlikable Michael is, but knows that he or at least his gift is her "strongest interest." The story she requests is not then, in any way, a romantic or personal one; it is an "account"; an account, not of Bristowe the man, but of his "strange career," that is, of the gift she believes him to have possessed.

Secondly, the story that Ralph tells—the heterosexual, couple-based romance between himself and Hilda with its predictable obstacle, the "other man"—is the very story Hilda consistently and explicitly rejects. Ralph suggests at the start that his marriage to Hilda is "a long-standing family plot." It is this plot which, as Ralph's mother senses when she hears about Hilda's "university career," Hilda will refuse, unravel, reject, and rewrite. Ralph implies throughout the novel that it is Hilda's interest in Michael which is keeping him from his "natural mate." He refuses, that is, to take seriously Hilda's own plot for her life. In the romantic narrative there are few things which can keep a man from his true love. Family opposition is one, but here there is family support. The obvious other is another man, and it is this plot element which Ralph seizes and exploits in his version of the story. The term "long-standing family plot," furthermore, suggests burial as well as wedding. In rejecting Ralph, Hilda rejects not only the families' plans but her place in the graveyard at the end of a life as dutiful daughter and wife, a life which would require her to bury her own needs and desires. All three plots—the grave, the plan, and the story-line—she recognises as attempts to entrap her, to take away her independent existence, to make her into a Viking princess in her father's hall. In contrast to the family plot and father's hall, Hilda's residences emphasise her status as independent woman. She begins in a Bloomsbury flat and moves with Michael to a cottage of her choosing after realising that Marling has no place for her and her chief interest. In both places she is, as Ralph notes with some chagrin, "very much upon her own ground" as opposed to being in or on the family plot.

Hilda's first explicit rejection of the plots occurs with Ralph's marriage proposal, which takes place, as does much of the story, on Hilda's ground. She is neither shocked or thrilled by the proposal, but considers it with rational detachment. No, she says, "she did not want to marry at present... she was keenly interested in her work... she was enjoying her life of independence in London, and had no desire for the ties of domesticity." Though Ralph records her answer, the most salient point he infers is that at least he has no "fears of a rival." He has earlier tried to dissuade her from seeing too much of the disreputable Michael. She makes very clear not only that she will not take his advice, but that "it might be the worst sort of crime one can commit if I did not help him." Since Ralph's response is to absent himself for a while and then to return to give her, as he says, another interest—himself and his renewal of the marriage proposal—he sets himself up as Michael's "rival" though Hilda assures him that Michael is not a rival and though he seems to accept that assurance. Ralph repeats the romantic story even when it is groundless.

Hilda's refusal to marry Ralph is a rational one. She does not reject marriage altogether: "she had no special feeling against it," but she rejects it only for herself, only at this time. Ralph's unwarranted, irrational inference here is that he has permission to persist in his suit. She asserts her interest in her work; this above all Ralph resents and refuses to take seriously. In fact, it is this interest, this "chief pretext for remaining unmarried," that, reassured about Michael, he sees as his best target for attack. His approach is silly and predictable. "You can't like working for Mrs. Hastings... Women always bully women. Everyone knows that." Again, Ralph adheres to an old story, and Hilda denies it in order to tell her own: "Some do and some don't... just like men. Mrs. Hastings is very pleasant to work for." Like the marriage and family plot, this story may be sometimes true, but not in this case, not for her. It is at this point that Ralph leaves "in impotent rage": Hilda, the rational woman, insists, simply and clearly, on shaping her own story and thus ruins his. Later, when Hilda tells Ralph that she is going to marry Michael, Ralph returns bitterly to the question of her work. He thinks he has discovered a hole in Hilda's story. Work "had been a sufficient reason for refusing to consider marriage with me; it apparently had no weight against the necessity of nursing Michael Bristowe." Again, Ralph believes that his story is the true one: women willingly give up their work for marriage or for nursing men. But again, it is Ralph's story which is wrong. He discovers later that Mrs. Hastings was, in fact, "keeping the post open for her." Hilda has no intention of abandoning her work; she only wants to devote herself for a time to a limited project which seems to her of enormous significance.

When Ralph leaves Hilda at the end of the novel, furthermore, she has engaged a nurse for the baby and expects "to be back at work again in a few weeks' time." Little as he likes it,

Ralph cannot tell Hilda's story without her work, just as Hilda cannot tell her own story without it. It establishes her identity at the beginning of the tale; she returns to it in the end; it comes up in conjunction with both Ralph's marriage proposals. Though Ralph attempts again and again to minimise its importance, its appearance at crucial points in the text works against his claim.

Refusal of the marriage proposals and insistence on work, whether political or personal, are both attempts on the part of Hilda and the text itself to deny the romantic story that Ralph keeps trying to tell. A third attempt is Hilda's consistently unromantic attitude toward Ralph, toward other men, and even toward the man she marries. Ralph complains early in the novel, for example, that Hilda treats him "as an old friend with whom a possible future business arrangement had been left temporarily in abeyance." At the end of the novel, as we have seen, she writes to him for financial help because he is "the nearest thing to a brother" that she has. The "warmest" comment she makes to him is, "It's pleasant to know that you want me, Ralph." Her regard for Ralph as an old friend, as a brother, as a partner in the enterprise that is her chief interest, indicates clearly that Ralph's romantic story is a fictional account, not because Ralph is either novelist or conscious deceiver but because he is himself entrapped in the romantic plot. Though he tries to find hints of some more romantic interest on Hilda's part, though he attempts to see Michael as a romantic rival, he must admit that Hilda is less "sex-conscious" than any other woman he has met. When he takes her to his club for dinner, he cannot decide whether it is "admirable" or "pathetic" that "she was obviously utterly unconscious of the discreetly admiring glances of my fellow-clubsmen." He responds here as predictably as Doctor Bays in *Ashley Hamel*, a novel by Somervillian Hilda Reid: "He had been scandalised earlier that morning by the advertisement of a seductive woman, but the sight of a woman who practised no seductive arts shocked him more profoundly still." Doctor Bays and Ralph, two educated men, cannot use their own intellectual tools to overcome the prejudices so deeply embedded in the romance plot that writes their lives.

Hilda herself says explicitly that she has a different plot in mind for her own life. "I've never been in love… the way books describe it. I think, that I am probably not capable of that." The books describe something Ralph and others seem to understand but she does not. Their plots and experiences are not hers. What shocks Ralph most, however, is not that she is not "in love" with him or is impervious to the romantic feelings she inspires in others but that she is not in love with the man she intends to marry. Though as Hilda points out, Ralph has himself defended "the French *mariage de convenance*," he finds similar sentiments in a woman incredible and unwomanly. Hilda's comment reveals Ralph's own irrationality and unquestioning adherence to the convention that marriage, while a pleasant and desirable addition to a man's already mildly successful and amusing life, is for a woman the "supreme experience of her sex."

Hilda's most open rejection of Ralph's romance is her expression of surprise that "I should ever hear you talk like a best-seller." Hilda's use of the derogatory "best-seller" rather than simply "book" implies that Ralph's story is a more thoroughgoing and less well-intentioned fiction than an ordinary novel. She here sees through Ralph's hypocrisy and his histrionic, irrational attempt to make her change her mind about marrying Michael. He speaks of the "horror" of a marriage without love, as though the tale he spins is not just romance but gothic romance, forgetting, but perhaps enacting, the gothic insight that it is most often the erotic which generates the honour. Hilda, the educated, rational woman, refuses to attend to his warning. The inflated rhetoric of the conclusion—the speculation on what Hilda has learned, Ralph's sense of Hilda as "desperately… clinging to the hope that her sacrifice had not been in vain"—must be seen in the light of this gothic rhetoric, in light of Hilda's perception that Ralph is talking like a best-seller. What he has written down is not the story Hilda asked him to tell, but a best-seller, a gothic romance that casts Hilda as properly chastened by the disastrous results of her Faustian, Frankensteinian "inadmissible enterprise." Ralph then writes himself off on a romantic expedition, having rejected the now awakened, no longer innocent woman, having, like the uninvited crone, cursed the newborn child under pretence of blessing her: "I cannot help suspecting that it may be the happiest thing for little Stella if she turns out, after all, to be completely commonplace."

Unable to "share a happy and normal life" with Hilda, unable, that is, to succeed in turning Hilda's story into a romance, Ralph hopes for a romantic script for Stella. Hilda, on the other hand, wants her daughter to have Michael's gift, to have it "in a higher degree than Michael." Again, we see the conflict between Ralph's plot and Hilda's; again we note that Hilda's breaks new ground. Like the American who, Ralph asserts, is "capable of seeing freshly without preconception," the educated woman has a vision. Unlike the American, who sees freshly only for his own profit, Hilda harbours ambitions for her child that centre not on her own gratification, not even on Stella's future, but on the good of all humanity, "a chance that may never come again." While, then, Ralph's plot is a romance, Hilda's is a vision; his is personal, hers social; his is conservative, hers adventurous, "an adventure of the race."

Finally, it is by the sex of child that the text significantly alters the romantic plot, and by her response to the sex of her child that Hilda definitively breaks into Ralph's romance. According to Ralph, Hilda herself had never considered the possibility that the inheritor of the gift would be female. "Master of Arts as she was, and as much of a feminist as are most educated women nowadays, Hilda, like any Victorian, had attached her exceptional hopes to a young prince." The text, however, has prepared the ground for the child's sex by the reference to von Reichenbach, a nineteenth-century German scientist, and his discovery of "a new sense in human beings." Unfortunately no one paid attention to his work because his most gifted subjects were "invalid girls." Stella, too, is an invalid girl: she is ill for weeks after birth, "small," "helpless," "pathetic" and she is in-valid because she is a girl. In Hilda's mental plot, at least as much of it as we can glean from Ralph's derisive summary, Hilda, the almost-virgin "Madonna" will bear a "young prince," a Messiah whose path she has made smooth. To conform to its Biblical analogue, the expected child should have been a son. But unlike Ralph, who cannot change his plot to accommodate new information, Hilda is able to turn her invalid girl into a valid messiah and to turn the biblical narrative into a modern story.

She names the child Stella, as "star" an indication both of the continued connection with the Christmas narrative and of the departure from it. She rejects the plot of motherhood to return to work, leaving Stella in the charge of "a highly trained nurse." Contrary to Ralph's allegation that Hilda has an aversion to Stella because of her sex, Hilda seems clearly to have made the adjustment in her expectations. "Do you see?" she asks Ralph "in an almost awe-stricken whisper," "she's trying to get her hands free." Miss Platt denies Ralph's explanation of Hilda's indifference to the child when she notes that Ralph is "upset, like most men, when they find that all women haven't the maternal instincts of a broody hen." And Hilda's reverential awe belies even the indifference. Further, the struggling hands of the child imply that, like her father, she will use her hands to "feel," as instruments of her sixth sense. The "trying to get her hands free" suggests also that as a female child she, like her mother, will refuse to be trapped by the romantic plot and will, unlike von Reichenbach's invalid girls, use her gift in a positive, rational, and valid way. Though Stella may inherit her father's gift of seeing beneath the surface, it is her mother who is her real creator, who will make sure that the child has "a better chance than poor Michael," that she does not "start with everything against [her]." In this revision of the Christmas story the mother takes the initiative to produce the new messiah, since in the post-war world "our God is one who needs our help." The death of the father and the investment of hope in the daughter emphasise the newness of this narrative.

At the end of the novel we see, with Ralph, a Hilda exhausted by her undertaking, alone, subdued. Unlike Ralph, however, we do not see her ruled now by fear and need; we do not see her as a failure. Ralph is quick to make these judgments yet has no ground for his pessimism but his own desire for feminine mediocrity for both mother and daughter. Though he consoles himself with the "incipient fulfilment of [his] prophecies," his own failure to participate when invited in what the text invites us to see as a messianic, evolutionary experiment has itself made Hilda's project more difficult than it need have been. He could not relinquish the romantic plot; he abandons Hilda after her marriage and is no longer interested in his "natural mate" once she has acted contrary to his wishes, once she has married, however briefly, however practically, another man. Theoretically supportive of women's higher education, Ralph is as frightened and horrified of its consequences as its opponents are. His setting off, at the end of the narrative, on an expedition, is flight as well as male adventure. He takes refuge in the masculine prerogative of foreign travel and novel excitement while Hilda, the real adventurer, goes quietly back to her work with Mrs. Hastings and to her evolutionary task. Ralph continues to write his romantic tale; he renounces his love for fallen Hilda and moves into another romantic adventure, while Hilda, the rational woman, continues to rewrite the conventional tale. If, as Ralph thinks, she could now accept his proposal, it would be as companion and friend that she would marry him; she arranges rationally for child care; no story of maternal instincts prompts her to give up her work even though the child is a very special one.

Although Hilda constantly revises Ralph's romantic narrative, she does not herself write or have an interest in writing. That task she gives over, too trustingly, to Ralph, the professional, with the request that he write the account of Michael Bristowe's strange career. Ralph cannot, however, write this account because it is not his story. In fact, the text suggests that Ralph senses that an account of Michael Bristowe would be not the story of a man at all but a testament to the creativity of an educated woman. Ralph watches the development of Michael with great anxiety, in part because the gift itself frightens him, but more because of Hilda's creative role in it. "It frightened me," he admits, "to remember that Hilda had deliberately helped to develop it, so that its potentiality had become infinitely greater than they [*sic*] need have been." It is Hilda, then, who has taken a simple enough gift of physical discernment and worked systematically to improve and expand it. To Ralph's romantic mind, the creation has taken on, like Frankenstein's experiment, a life of its own "half wizard and half monster," has become "a live menacing entity." Hilda is, then, a powerful if unconscious creator whose material is not words on paper but the stuff of the human race; she is not Ralph's serving goddess, but a creator god/goddess; Michael Bristowe's story is, in this very concrete way, her own. Her decision to reproduce Michael's gift and Michael's story can be seen, of course, as her acceptance of the womanly role. Even her motives, while not sexually romantic, are altruistic and self-denying in the way that the romance plot conventionally dictates the good woman's motives to be. Three things, however, work against this interpretation. One is the very feminine nature of Michael and Michael's gift. Although his sense begins as something sex-neutral, an ability to detect the presence of metals and various objects, with Hilda's encouragement and tutoring it becomes an ability to sense people, both their presence and their motives, and to communicate in some intuitive, wordless way. The sixth sense, in other words, is very like "women's intuition"; Michael himself is stereotypically feminine. Helpless, unambitious, sickly, moody, he welcomes Hilda's taking charge of his life.

Thus Hilda devotes her energy not to a romantic man but to a weak and irritating one, not to a man's gift but to a woman's.

Second is Hilda's clear sense of her mission's limits. She knows that Michael will not live long. She even asks her employer to hold her job. Far from the all-encompassing and life-long commitment demanded by the romance, Hilda's commitment is circumscribed and temporary. Third is Ralph's own acknowledgment of Hilda's role in Michael's gift and life. He believes she has saved Michael's life; he believes she has created this "half wizard and half monster." Ralph can give no reason for his sinister interpretation of Michael's sixth sense; perhaps its very association with the feminine frightens him. Aside from Ralph's rhetoric, the sense appears valuable and fairly congenial. Although readers have no grounds for adopting Ralph's attitude toward the gift, his account of its development seems reliable enough: it is as much Hilda's creation as Michael's potential. Her decision to reproduce can be seen as the decision to continue, despite Ralph's warnings and objections, her own plot line. Ralph acknowledges this in an extravagant simile at the end of the tale when he asserts that someone who "tries to practise ideals in this world is like one who composes an Ode to Peace while the enemy is setting fire to the Thatch." We could turn Ralph's simile on himself and see him as the idealist whose project/plot—both of marrying Hilda and of writing her romance—is set fire to by Hilda, the subverter, like Bronte's fire-wielding Bertha, of traditional values and of traditional texts.

In Ralph's text, though, the idealist is of course Hilda, the educated woman, who in the simile takes on the dimensions of a composer or poet whose work is continually subverted by "the enemy." Such subversion is easy if the enemy appears as friend, and Ralph's own role has become that of the enemy in the guise of supporter and friend, the man who, unlike "many of my contemporaries... [has] never been against the higher education of women." Nevertheless, he subverts Hilda's efforts, in large part because he does not want Hilda to succeed in her creation, in what the text sees as her daring enterprise. What he wants is to settle down with her as princess of his hall; by setting fire to her Thatch he hopes to smoke her out of her own territory and into his—a kind of manuscript-burning, which he is too civilised and rational to do in reality, but which he effectively accomplishes by turning her story into his own romance. Only when the reader recognises the enemy in friend's clothing does Hilda's story emerge and does the ending reflect not, as Ralph would have it, a woman punished for refusal to play her proper part, but a woman, like Jaeger's Sand, "immensely courageous and highly vocal," who makes people freer because she "explored the uncleared country for them."

Jaeger's juxtaposition of a secular, female-centred nativity narrative with a thwarted tale of romance becomes her strategy for circumventing the romantic plot. She portrays the educated woman as trapped by the text, trapped by the romantic story the narrator wants to tell. By providing another layer, however, a tale of origins and destinies, a tale, moreover, which revises and reverses that myth, both etiological and teleological, of Christianity, Jaeger allows her heroine to slip out of the more literary text and into the mythic one, in which elements of romance diffuse themselves in confrontation with the sacred. Although the sacred here is secular, the other-worldly this-worldly, the powerful father-god a weak human man, the submissive woman a powerful mother-creator, the male saviour a female star, tiny, weak, but growing, the effect and significance remain the same: next to the blueprint for the future of the human race, the heterosexual romance pales. No rhetoric on the part of the narrator can inflate that plot to comparable proportions.

The Oxbridge education sets in motion this shift from plot to myth and epic because it replaces shyness with confidence, submission with initiative, fairy tale with reason—in other words, powerlessness with power. The romantic plot is, for women, the origin and embodiment of powerlessness. Trapped in it, women only repeat it. One way out, Jaeger's text suggests, is through the uncleared country of originary myth where women can start over, this time with education and power on their side.

SUSAN J. LEONARDI

CLASSIC LITERARY SCIENCE FICTION
BY MURIEL JAEGER

In 1925 Muriel Jaeger, dissatisfied with the unrealistic utopian stories of H.G. Wells and Edward Bellamy, set out to explore 'The Question Mark' of what a future society might look like if human nature were truthfully represented.

Her hero, disgruntled office worker Guy, is pitched 200 years into a future London where each citizen is offered free education and a personal 'power-box' granting access to communication, transportation and entertainment. To Guy, the great challenges facing society seem solved, but its inhabitants tell a different story of fractured life in this supposed utopia.

Preceding the publication of Huxley's *Brave New World* by five years, *The Question Mark* is a significant cornerstone in the foundation of the dystopia genre, and an impressive work of literary science fiction.

CLASSIC LITERARY SCIENCE FICTION
BY IAN MACPHERSON

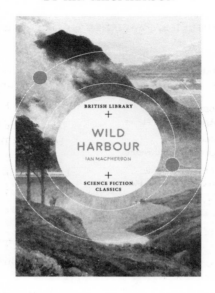

15 May 1944 – This morning I said to Terry,
'I thought I heard guns through the night.'
'Were you awake too?' she asked.

Something has happened in Europe. Fearing the approach of war to
Britain, Terry and Hugh retreat from their home to the remote high-
lands of Scotland, prepared to live a simple existence together whilst
the fighting resolves itself far away.

Encouraged by Terry, Hugh begins a journal to note down the highs
and lows of this return to nature, and to process their concerns of the
oncoming danger. But as the sound of guns by night grow louder, the
grim prospect of encroaching war threatens to invade their cherished
isolation and demolish any hope of future peace.

Macpherson's speculative novel of future war was first published in 1936,
just 3 years before the outbreak of the Second World War in Europe.

BRITISH LIBRARY SCIENCE FICTION CLASSICS

SHORT STORY ANTHOLOGIES
EDITED BY MIKE ASHLEY

Lost Mars:
The Golden Age of the Red Planet

Moonrise:
The Golden Age of Lunar Adventures

Menace of the Machine:
The Rise of AI in Classic Science Fiction

The End of the World
and Other Catastrophes

Menace of the Monster:
Classic Tales of Creatures from Beyond

Beyond Time:
Classic Tales of Time Unwound

Born of the Sun:
Adventures in Our Solar System

CLASSIC SCIENCE
FICTION NOVELS

By William F Temple

Shoot at the Moon
Four-Sided Triangle

By Charles Eric Maine

The Tide Went Out
The Darkest of Nights

By Ian Macpherson

Wild Harbour

By Muriel Jaeger

The Question Mark
The Man with Six Senses

We welcome any suggestions, corrections or feedback you may have, and will aim to respond to all items addressed to the following:

The Editor (Science Fiction Classics)
British Library Publishing
The British Library
96 Euston Road
London, NW1 2DB

We also welcome enquiries through our Twitter account, @BL_Publishing.